The Mixed-Up Summer of Lily McLean

Kelpies is an imprint of Floris Books
First published in 2015 by Floris Books
© 2015 Lindsay Littleson

Lindsay Littleson has asserted her right under the
Copyright, Designs and Patent Act 1988 to be
identified as the Author of this work.

This publisher acknowledges subsidy from
Creative Scotland towards the publication
of this volume

MIX
Paper from
responsible sources
FSC® C117931

This book is also available as an eBook

British Library CIP data available
ISBN 978-178250-180-0
Printed & Bound by MBM Print SCS Ltd, Glasgow

The Mixed-Up Summer of Lily McLean

Lindsay Littleson

 Kelpies

To Mum and Dad,
With love and thanks for all your support.
You were right... bad times don't last.

Chapter 1

Today's really weird events:

- ★ My sister explodes.
- ★ I get a free holiday.
- ★ We don't find a rat. (It's much worse than that!)

"You can't force me! I won't go! You can't dump me on a boggin' desert island and leave me there for a week!"

My sister Jenna is working herself up to a complete nuclear meltdown.

"I just asked if you would like to go to Millport on a wee holiday with your gran, Jenna. Nobody's dumping you anywhere," snaps Mum.

This is bad. Mum is losing patience. Jenna's about to blow. I could get hit by flying shrapnel.

The Isle of Cumbrae isn't my idea of a desert island. It's less than ten minutes on the ferry from the mainland for a start. And it has a town, Millport, and proper tarmac roads, cafés and an amusement arcade. So it isn't exactly a shipwrecked-like-Robinson-Crusoe situation, is it?

"Mum, this is so unfair! Jessica is going to Spain for her holidays. Sarah's parents are taking her camping in France," wails Jenna. "And you expect me to be happy with freaking Millport! I hate you! I'm not going! There isn't even wi-fi! I can't get decent reception on my mobile! I'll be completely cut off!"

You'd think it was a zillion mega-miles from civilisation the way Jenna carries on. Her wailing and bawling would embarrass a three year old. And she's fifteen.

"I'm not going! I am absolutely not going and you can't make me! No way am I spending a week in (insert your own choice of swear word here, because I'm not telling you hers) Millport!" she shrieks. My sister's tantrums are spectacular. I am in total awe sometimes.

At other times, I wish she'd grow up. I'm four years younger and I feel loads more mature.

Jenna screams hideously, at higher decibels than the silly girls in her beloved vampire movies, and throws a cushion, which bounces off the table lamp and knocks it over. The lamp tumbles on to the carpet, denting the shade. Mum loses her temper. Her face is going very red. This is really not good.

"Jenna, will you calm down right now! Don't you dare damage the furniture!" she yells.

"How can I calm down when you're trying to ruin my life? This is so unfair!" howls Jenna.

I flick a glance at the school photo on the mantelpiece: Jenna aged twelve, her hair in two neat blonde plaits, a big toothy grin and smiley blue eyes. I look at her now: purple streaks in her dyed black hair, thick eyeliner and face contorted with fury. What happened to my big sister?

For a millisecond I consider joining in the battle on Mum's side, but decide it would be futile, maybe even dangerous, to point out to Jenna that a week's holiday in Millport is hardly likely to ruin her life. (Only a week of it, max.)

I start to edge slowly towards the door, afraid that if either of them notices me, I might be drawn unwillingly into the fight. I don't share Jenna's love of confrontation.

Perfectly timed with Jenna's next eruption, I slip out and retreat towards the safety of the cupboard.

You don't need to feel sorry for me. I don't *live* in the cupboard. I'm not Harry flippin' Potter. But I like my own space, and space is hard to come by in our house. If there was such a thing as a national minimum space standard, our house would have a big 'Not Fit for Purpose' sticker stuck on the front door.

You couldn't swing a cat, let alone the six of us, in this house (or so my mum shouted at the council guy who showed us around). You'd need to be a major psychopath to swing a cat, though, wouldn't you? I read somewhere that psychopaths always start with cats.

I like cats, honestly. We have two, McTavish and Quipp, named after the firm of lawyers who fleeced my mum during her last divorce.

That sounds bad, as if Mum divorces a lot. She's only done it twice. So there are two ex-husbands: my dad and my step-dad, although my dad is particularly ex because he's dead. My step-dad is very much alive, and making my mum's life harder than it needs to be, she says.

For now, though, our house is enough of a war zone without worrying about him. Jenna's words are bouncing off the walls like grenades.

I creep stealthily, like a burglar, towards the cupboard and turn the door handle. If I move quickly, I should manage to get in completely unnoticed.

"I am not going to Millport! You might as well just kill me now! I hate you and I hate this stupid house!" she screams.

Mum's replies are machine-gun staccato. And suddenly, adding to the din, there's a deafeningly high-pitched wail like an air raid siren.

"Mum! Bronx has the remote and he won't give it to

me and I don't want to watch Ben 10. I want to watch the Spiderman DVD. Mum! It's not fair! Mum!"

Oh great. Now Hudson has joined in. Let World War Three commence.

The fact that I have a hideout in the cupboard is not information I wish to share with my family. It's a secret, but not the biggest secret I am keeping.

I switch on the cupboard light and creep inside, shutting the door quietly on the racket.

Now I have some peace, I reflect on our lack of living space. My mum has her bedroom upstairs, which my baby sister Summer sleeps in too. My older sister Jenna has a tiny room not much bigger than this cupboard, all to herself (because nobody in their right mind would want to share with her), and I sleep in the third bedroom with my two wee brothers, Bronx and Hudson. They are six and seven and sleep in bunk beds, which they fight over on a nightly basis. They fight over everything. They are fighting at this very moment.

"Bronx, if you don't give me that remote, I'm going to get a bazooka and blow you into a squillion bits!"

"Mum! Hudson's being horrible to me!" squeals Bronx. "I need to watch Ben 10 and he won't let me!"

"Shut up, you little morons!" shouts Jenna, at exactly

the same time as Mum yells at Bronx and Hudson to be quiet. At least they agree about something.

I hate sharing a room, particularly with small, noisy, smelly boys, and I am finding it very difficult to get used to our new sleeping arrangements. We had much more space in the house we lived in before. Sorry, I am starting to sound as spoiled and whiney as Jenna. Whoops.

I'm not the only one who hates the house though. Mum does the lottery every week, desperate to win enough to buy a bigger house. My gran says it's a ridiculous waste of money, which is a bit of a cheek, as she plays bingo whenever she gets the chance.

"If you loved me, you wouldn't ask me to do this!" wails Jenna, her voice muffled a bit by the closed cupboard door. "Millport is only fun for ancient people like Gran and wee kids like Lily. This is so unfair!"

Wee kids like me, huh. But who's having the toddler tantrum, Jenna?

Just a couple of years ago, Jenna thought it was the best thing ever to leave Mum, Bronx, Hudson and Summer behind and head off on the ferry with me and Gran for a week in a rented caravan in Millport.

We'd scramble about in the rock pools carrying plastic buckets and fishing nets, hunting for minnows and tiny crabs. We would cycle round the island on hired bikes and buy ice lollies from the Fintry Bay café. We'd dare each other to dip our toes in the freezing sea and if the weather was even remotely warm, we would risk an icy swim. If it was wet, and being a Scottish island it often poured for days on end, we would play cards or Monopoly in the caravan or venture out to the Ritz café for a hot chocolate. I loved those holidays and Jenna did too. But not any more she doesn't. Now Millport is the end of the world, according to my big, thinks-she's-so-grown-up sister.

"Mum, Hudson spilled juice all over the carpet!" screeches Bronx.

"I have not spilled it, you pushed me and you knocked it out of my hand!"

Mum abandons the battle with Jenna for a moment and rushes through to the kitchen to grab a wad of kitchen roll.

"For goodness' sake boys, is the carpet not disgusting enough already without this mess!" She's not wrong there.

"It wasn't me!" wails Hudson, who never accepts blame for anything, even when he's caught red-handed.

I think he only knows three phrases: "Bronx made me do it," "It wasn't me!" and "He started it."

I know the wee ones have weird names. I blame my step-dad. He's a nutter. He called the boys after places in New York, even though he's never been there. In fact he prides himself on never having left Ayrshire in his whole life. I bet you're thinking that my mum should have put her foot down about the names – she was there at the birth after all. But you don't know my step-dad. People don't cross him.

Well, we did cross him in the end, but that's another story. I might tell it later, but I kind of prefer not to talk about it as a rule. It wasn't a happy time.

Maybe that's what's wrong with my sister. Perhaps she's got post-traumatic stress disorder or something. I read about that somewhere. Mum says I've not to be daft and it's hormones that are making Jenna a nightmare. (She says I'll be as bad in a year or so, but I refuse to believe that I will ever be that unreasonable.)

Not that Jenna's like that when she's with her silly friends though. She's a different person then, all hair tossing and eyelash fluttering and giggling and eyeing up boys. No, she keeps her true nightmarish personality for her own family. We're the ones who suffer.

Their voices are louder, less muffled now. The fight has clearly moved from the living room into the hall.

"I never get my own way about anything," weeps Jenna.

"Well let me see," says Mum. "What about the time you wanted to go to a festival and I said no, and you went anyway?"

"Yeah, but you were just being mean saying no. Jess was allowed to go. Her mum's not a cow. And nothing bad happened did it?"

"You're hardly going to tell me otherwise, Jenna," snaps Mum.

"It was just one time!" roars Jenna. "Get over it!"

"And what about the time you pierced your nose?" I mutter, glad Jenna can't hear me. I'd never dare to say these things to her face.

I hear a creak and know that Mum has just sat down on the stairs, a sure sign that she is admitting defeat.

"Why can't you do something just to please your old gran?" Mum asks, in a hopeless attempt to make Jenna feel guilty. "Lily isn't making this fuss!"

"That's because Lily's a sanctimonious little creep! She's a smarmy little goody two-shoes!"

Oh, that's charming. Thanks for that, sis. Sometimes I wish my cupboard had soundproofing. I stick my earphones in my ears and crank my radio up.

"That's a very unkind thing to say about your sister, Jenna!" snaps Mum, kindly leaping to my defence.

"You don't know what she's like when you're out at work. She's always making trouble for me with Gran!"

This is so unfair that my jaw drops. It's not my fault that Gran finds Jenna a major handful at the moment. It's not my fault she prefers me. I am tempted to fling myself out of the cupboard and rugby tackle Jenna to the floor. But then they would know I was in here and I would much prefer to keep my hiding place a secret.

Mum works most days as a cleaner. She does another early evening shift selling ice cream in a café on the front, near the pier, but that's seasonal. Gran babysits for the wee ones when Mum's at work, which is good because Mum doesn't need to pay her, but Mum says that actually she pays *dearly* for it. I can see what she means. Gran knows fine well that Mum needs her, and she likes the power it gives her. Gran is actually my dad's mum. Mum's own parents moved down South to sunny Brighton when they retired, and who can blame them? It rains here in Largs all the bloomin' time.

A door slams. Then another. Above the tinny music on my radio, I can hear Bronx and Hudson wailing.

"Mummmmm, Hudson hit me with the remote. It's not fair!"

"He nipped me first, Mum! And Mum, Summer stinks! I think she's got a dirty nappy!"

I turn the knob on my radio up and the DJ's inane rabbiting is finally all I can hear. It's a major improvement.

Where was I? Oh yeah, our space issue – there's also a tiny galley kitchen, which can only hold two people at a time, at a push. Mum does the 'cooking' (if heating up ready meals in the microwave counts as cooking), but Jenna is quite good at it when she is in a giving mood, which is increasingly rare. She makes us all spaghetti carbonara or bolognaise and leaves the kitchen looking like the aftermath of a major natural disaster.

Finally, there's the living room, which is in dire need of a 60-minute makeover. It has a swirly lime-green carpet, floral-patterned peach curtains and lumpy textured wallpaper. It's in here that Bronx and Hudson watch cartoons and play Xbox and fight with each other, while baby Summer howls in her playpen and Mum and I try and eat our dinner and hear the television above the racket. Jenna takes her plate into her room and rarely brings the dirty ones back out. Mum says we'll get rats.

I daren't tell her it's much worse than that. We've got a disembodied voice in the house.

Chapter 2

Ways to freak out my mum:

- ⭐ Lie very still on the hall carpet.
- ⭐ Scream like you're on fire.
- ⭐ Tell her you're hearing voices. (On second thoughts, don't.)

On a typical weekday evening Mum leaves work about five o'clock, looking frazzled, and picks us up from Gran's house on her way home. Baby Summer will be tired, hungry and fractious after her day at nursery.

Mum will take one step through the door and Jenna will have flown into a sulk because Mum has "smiled sarcastically" or just existed, really, and within seconds they will be screaming at each other and doors will be slamming and little kids will be wailing. Most days I try and help by bribing the boys with television or by reading stories. I unofficially borrow books I think they will enjoy from our school library, sit Summer on my knee and read aloud to the three of them. Their favourite is *Peace at Last* by Jill Murphy. They like joining in with all the noises… particularly the aeroplane one! I don't think I'm going to get round to taking that one back to the library. But sometimes, particularly after a hard day at school, all the arguments and the screaming feel too much to stand, and I will back away quietly and head for the hall cupboard.

The cupboard is my haven, my get-away-from-it-all place. It has an electric light, which is handy, as I don't love the dark, particularly since I read one of those vampire books my sister left lying in the bathroom. Most of it was sick-making romantic guff, but there was a really scary bit and I can't stop remembering the scratching fingers and chalk-white vampire faces when the lights go out at night.

I share this cosy space with a vacuum cleaner and a rather stale-smelling mop and bucket, both of which smell sweeter than Hudson and Bronx. But stuffed right at the back, where nobody will spot it, there's a small wicker basket. Inside the basket there's a stack of books and magazines, a tiny portable radio Mum gave me last Christmas, and a notebook and pen.

I bought the notebook with my Christmas money from Gran and it's nearly full. I write poetry in my notebook, and sometimes stories, and most days, lists. I love lists. I have a lot to remember and they help me to stay organised. I don't call my notebook a diary because then I'd feel under pressure to write a lot every day, and sometimes that's just not possible. But there's always time for a list.

When I grow up, I want to be a famous author, or perhaps a lawyer, because they are mega-loaded. No way am I being poor like my mum.

I keep a cushion in the basket too, which I 'borrowed' from Jenna's room. It's purple and fluffy, and has sequins spelling out the word LOVE, which would be mega-mortifying if my pals saw it, but Rowan and David are never here so it isn't a worry. My cupboard will stay top secret, even from them.

My friend David's house has three bedrooms like mine, but a lot fewer kids to cram into it. And they have two bathrooms and a kitchen that my whole house would fit into quite nicely. You could swing several cats in there, maybe even a puma or a leopard. And he has a big bedroom all to himself, painted cobalt blue – David was very specific about it being *cobalt* blue. When I was at his place, I was mega-jealous of everything in it, except his enormous collection of Star Wars memorabilia. He can keep that.

David's dad is an accountant and his mum's a teacher and they go somewhere like Turkey or Menorca every summer for a fortnight. I'll bet Jenna would not be carrying on like this if Gran had suggested Menorca instead of Millport, internet connection or not. She would be upstairs packing her case right now.

I take my earphones out to check that my crazy family haven't chosen today, a long, dull Sunday, to kill each other or something. I'd seriously have to intervene then.

"Jenna, come out your room right now! You can't stay in there forever, madam! We need to discuss this calmly!"

My mum is sounding a long way from calm. There's no reply from Jenna, but I can hear a squeaky battle going on between Bronx and Hudson over control of the remote, and Summer is wailing loudly.

"It's my turn. Gimme it!"

"No way, you watched three programmes yesterday and I only got to watch one. Mummmm, Hudson took the batteries out!"

Excellent, everyone's still alive. I put my earphones back in and go back to thinking about David, who isn't going to be invited to my house any time soon. Even though I'm sure he wouldn't sneer at the mess. He has nice manners, drilled into him by his mum, who teaches gym, so that tells you what she's like. And David isn't the tidiest person himself. His hair is always sticking up at funny angles, as though he has slept on it, and his clothes look permanently dishevelled and ill fitting, probably because he is a bit of a tricky shape. David is shorter than the average eleven-year-old boy, a fact which worries him a lot, and he's a little overweight, which doesn't bother him at all.

But I wouldn't want to watch him stepping over the broken toys and dirty laundry and the pushchair in the hall. And then where would we go? We wouldn't get any peace in the cramped pigsty of a bedroom I share with Hudson and Bronx. And I wouldn't want to take him into our cluttered, untidy living room. Even the newish table lamp has a bash in it now, thanks to Jenna's latest meltdown. Nope, it's not happening.

And Rowan's parents won't let her through the door of my house. Her mum came round to our old house in Kelvin Street one evening last October. I think she was selling tickets for the PTA Halloween disco or something. My step-dad had started early on the vodka. He was totally off his face and pretty unpleasant.

Rowan has explained repeatedly to her mum that my step-dad has gone for good, but she is still not allowed to visit, which is fine with me, even if I'm mortified by the reason for it.

So, at this precise moment, I'm in the cupboard in the hall, earplugs in and the radio blaring, reading *Anne of Green Gables* for the umpteenth time. Anne always says exactly what she's thinking, which both impresses and appals me, and I can totally sympathise with her red hair issues. The words are bouncing about on the page though, as they always do when I've got a headache, so I close the book and sit and think about my troublesome family.

Jenna is probably still stropping about being forced to go to Millport for her summer holidays, leaving her beloved 'bezzies' behind. Bronx and Hudson will be squabbling over the remote or sitting glassy-eyed on the couch, watching Sponge Bob or Scooby Doo. Summer might be wailing, because nobody is paying her any attention. If she is, I will go and pick her up and play with her for a wee while. Somebody has to and it isn't going to be Mum or Jenna at this rate. I put my book down, take my earphones out and listen intently.

The television is blaring, the boys are silent and I can hear Mum clattering about, obviously having given up on attempting to talk Jenna out of her room.

"Right, Summer," she says, sounding a bit grumpy and impatient. "Let's get that smelly nappy off."

"Not here, Mum!" yells Bronx. "Take her somewhere else! She stinks!"

"Don't say that," tuts Mum. "She can't help having a dirty nappy. You'll hurt her feelings."

"Summer hasn't got feelings, silly, she's only a baby! An ugly, buggly, stinky-poo baby!"

That's really mean, Bronx. Admittedly, Summer may have a permanently runny nose and stained hand-me-downs, but I think she's pretty cute. She has curly ginger hair, a freckly face and a snub nose, like Little Orphan Annie in the musical, if Orphan Annie had been shrunk in the wash. And had a permanently runny nose. But I am very fond of her. She smiles at me sunnily every time I pick her up and we've got to do something to make up for the fact that she's got the dad from hell.

I keep my earphones out, since it's quite peaceful now in the house, and make myself comfortable on my cushion. I lean back against the wall, pick up my book again and am trying to enjoy the quiet, when my cupboard door is flung open and daylight streams in. Can a person not get any peace? I poke my head out, but there's nobody in the hall. I can hear the television, and Mum clattering in the kitchen, and Summer banging a rattle against the wall of her playpen, happy to finally be wearing a clean nappy. Silence from Jenna. She has probably barricaded herself in her bedroom and is now messaging her friends, threatening to run away from home.

If only.

I pull the door shut and sit back down on that hideous cushion.

"I wish you were here, Lily."

I shoot into the air and bang my head on the electricity meter. Crumple back down on the floor, head throbbing and heart racing. Glance around, eyes wide. But there's definitely nobody there.

Then the light bulb pops. The cupboard instantly goes pitch black. I'm sitting in total darkness, my hand fumbling for the door handle, numb with fear, when I hear it again, right next to my ear.

"And I wish you could hear me, Lily," the voice whispers.

My hand finds the handle and I roll, Ninja-like, out of the cupboard and faceplant onto our garishly patterned hall carpet. I lie there for a moment, staring at the weird squiggly design, and waiting for my heart to stop leaping about in my chest. I'm scared that I'm having a heart attack, like old Mrs McInnes over the road.

When we visited her afterwards in the hospital, Mrs McInnes told Mum that it had felt like her heart was being squeezed in a vice. I'm not sure what that feels like, but it sounds sore, and as I calm down a bit, I realise I'm not actually in pain at all. It must just be a panic attack, brought on by extreme terror. A disembodied voice will do that to a person, especially when the disembodied voice knows your name.

I roll over on to my back and gaze up at the ceiling with its swirly loops of plaster. This house does not have restful décor. I try and gather my thoughts.

I'm hearing voices, is my first thought.

Well, just one voice, but that's quite crazy enough, thanks, is my second.

"Um, Lily, what are you doing?" asks Mum. She's

standing at the kitchen door, wiping her hands on a tea towel. "Why on earth are you lying on the floor?"

"No reason," I reply, trying to look nonchalant while lying on my back on the hall carpet. I haul myself upright and smile cheerfully. Hiding my real feelings is my area of expertise – I've had years of practice. "I was just checking for holes in the skirting boards. I heard scratching when I was walking through the hall and I thought I should check, just in case."

Mum's look of abject horror makes me wish I'd told her I'd simply gone mad instead. "Jenna!" she screeches at the closed bedroom door. "Get those dirty plates out of your room and into the sink! I told you we'd get rats!"

"I think I must have imagined the scratching," I break in hastily. "It was probably Bronx or Hudson carrying on in the living room. You know what they're like."

Mum looks uncertain. She clearly wants to believe that there are no rodents in the house, but needs a bit more persuasion. Then I have a brainwave.

"Mac and Quipp would have caught any rats or mice as soon as they dared show their little whiskery faces. You can tell Quipp's a great mouser just by watching him stalk spiders," I say firmly.

I see Mum visibly relax, and decide that distraction would be an excellent tactic at this point. Maybe I should be a lawyer, after all?

"So Mum, what's all the fuss about Millport?" I ask casually. "Jenna doesn't seem too thrilled," I add, with spectacular understatement.

"I knew Jenna wouldn't be keen to stay with Gran in a caravan this year. I did suggest Bronx and Hudson go instead of her, but Gran was having none of that. Mean old so and so."

I can see both sides of this story. I have a lot of sympathy with Gran, as a holiday in a caravan with Hudson and Bronx would be no holiday at all. And Gran loves her holidays in Millport. But for Mum, it would be an answer to a prayer. She would have a whole week without the gruesome twosome's constant squabbling.

"That's a shame," I say, although I don't sound terribly convincing. From a purely selfish point of view, I am completely on Gran's side on this one. I share a room with Bronx and Hudson all year. I would like some peace and privacy on my summer holiday too.

"So I was trying to persuade Jenna to go," says Mum with an exasperated sigh. "But she is dead against it. I'm not going to force her."

I wouldn't fancy Mum's chances of success, but if by some miracle she did manage to convince Jenna to go, it would be Gran and me who would suffer. It'd be the holiday from hell. She would make every minute miserable, with her sulks, tantrums and complaints. Now that I think about it, perhaps I'd rather have Bronx and Hudson. At least they would enjoy themselves.

"Gran will be disappointed if Jenna doesn't come," I say carefully.

I think I'm on safe ground here.

My gran dotes on Jenna and me, despite Jenna's recent transformation. She is not nearly so fond of the other three, which is sad for them, and sometimes a bit uncomfortable for us, particularly at Christmas and birthdays, when Gran's favouritism really shows (much to my mum's fury). The fact is, she's mine and Jenna's gran by blood, but not theirs – and while she looks out for *all* of us, I guess she can't hide her affection for her own son's daughters. Gran would be mortified if we said anything though.

Despite her love for Jenna, Gran isn't afraid to muscle in with the discipline. She says she needs a good smack. Mind you, Gran says that a lot, mostly in a big loud voice when she sees a kid misbehaving in the street or in a shop. It's mega-embarrassing.

"Listen to that cheeky wee so and so!" she bawled last weekend, when she and I were out getting her shopping. (She needs me to be her bag-carrier.) "If I'd spoken to my mother like that, she'd have boxed my ears!"

The child's mother whirled round and swore at my gran, who now felt completely justified.

"That explains everything," Gran said loudly as she flounced out, while I trailed behind, scarlet-faced and laden with plastic carrier bags. "Poor wee wean, having a mother so foul mouthed."

It was unimaginable humiliation. No wonder Jenna refuses to help Gran with the shopping.

So I am her favourite grandchild now, by a mile. I do as I'm told, say the right things and keep my thoughts firmly to myself.

"You can say no to this…" continues Mum, "but would you consider going to Millport on your own? Just you and Gran? If you think it would be really boring, I'm sure we could come up with a polite excuse."

I consider for all of one second.

"I'd love to go," I say, and I absolutely mean it. A week without my noisy siblings on an island I adore. It sounds like heaven.

Thinking about heaven reminds me that I am being haunted, or almost worse, am hearing imaginary voices in my head. It seems another very good reason for getting out of this house.

"When do I leave?" I ask happily. Mum looks a bit affronted and I think maybe I am overdoing my enthusiasm to get away from here. "I just wondered if Gran is planning to go during term time again," I add quickly, "because they don't love that at school."

"Last week of term, I think. You won't be doing any work by that point, will you?"

I guess that Mrs McKenzie would beg to differ, and I know for a fact that the last week of this term is a pretty significant one. It's my final week of primary school ever. At the end of the summer holidays I'll be starting secondary school. I feel really torn, but I'm not going to argue myself out of the only holiday I'm going to get this summer. And the realisation that I will miss the Leavers' Dance swings it. I really, really don't want to go to that dance.

"Great," I say, and I quickly do a countdown in my head. This time in two weeks, I'll be out of this house. And, hopefully, I'll be leaving the voice behind me. I need a break from *that*, more than anything else.

I haven't really explained the voice properly, have I? That's because I have no earthly idea what's going on. I just know it's terrifying; scarier than scratchy vampire fingers, because at least the vampires are outside the window, scratching to be let in, not right in the room beside you, whispering in your ear.

The whole haunting thing started about a month ago. In fact, it was on the 9th of May, which was Summer's birthday. We were all sitting around in the living room helping Summer open her presents, which wasn't hugely exciting for her, as she got a peach woolly cardigan and a pair of little flowery dungarees from Mum and a five-pack of white socks from Gran. Mum said she's too young to care what she's given for her birthday, but it seemed a bit mean to me. Though, to be fair, she was having the time of her life just tearing up the wrapping paper.

I had bought her a cuddly lion. Well, strictly speaking, I hadn't bought it for her, but I had put so many 20p coins into the grabber machine on the sea front that I might as well have gone into a shop and paid for a decent-looking toy lion, instead of the rather bedraggled creature I'd won. But you know that feeling when the metal grabber bit keeps letting go just as you think you've won and you become absolutely determined to get your hands on that particular toy, at whatever cost? Well, that's why Summer got a tatty orange lion with a fluorescent pink mane for her second birthday.

Summer ripped all of the spotty pink wrapping paper away and was delighted with it – the lion this time, not the wrapping paper. She cuddled her new toy tightly round its mangy fur tummy and chewed on its orange ears, which I presumed meant that she was pleased. I was feeling quite smug about the whole thing, cause I think Jenna had completely forgotten she even had a baby sister, never mind that it was her second birthday.

And then that voice whispered in my ear, just loud enough for me to hear.

"Why didn't you stay?"

I spun round as quickly as a Waltzer at the fair, but there was nobody there. I could see my entire family in front of me. The boys were sprawled on the swirly lime carpet and Gran, Mum and Jenna were perched on the couch. None of them was standing next to me, whispering in my ear. On a scale of zero to ten, with zero being totally ok and ten being a zombie invasion, it was about a seven.

Ever since, the voice has been getting more and more insistent. It only happens in the house, never at school, and it always takes me completely by surprise, like today's encounter in the cupboard.

"Lily, can you get the boys dressed before your gran comes over!" shouts Mum.

I sigh, and wander into the living room, preparing to haul the boys off the couch. It's the afternoon and they aren't even out of their pyjamas yet.

"Right lads, PJs off! Clothes on!" I shout.

Suddenly the voice speaks, quite loudly in my ear.

"Who said that? Who are you?" I scream like Jenna in a strop and Mum comes running. I have to pretend that Bronx kicked me when I was pulling him off the couch, which isn't very fair on Bronx. The poor wee soul doesn't even try and defend himself. Kicking people is an automatic reflex for him, so he probably believes he's actually done it. But what choice do I have? I'm afraid Mum will drag me off to the doctor for a brain scan or something. And the thing is, I really don't think that I'm imagining things.

I'm sure that I recognise the voice.

Chapter 3

Things I love about my baby sister:

* She has a cute laugh.
* She thinks I'm wonderful.
* She doesn't pee against walls.

I decide that hanging around the house doing nothing is not a productive way to spend a warmish Sunday afternoon and I can't possibly return to the cupboard until somebody changes the light bulb. What can I do?

I need to get out of here. I wrestle with the buggy in the hallway until eventually it unfolds. Then I pick up Summer from her playpen, stuff her chubby little arms into her anorak and plonk her into the buggy. She sits there looking up at me expectantly, clutching her tatty orange lion.

"We're going for a walk, Summer! That will be fun, won't it?"

She gets very excited, beams delightedly and makes some loud noises, which sound to me almost like words. Gran says she should be talking by now.

"That child clearly has developmental delay," I heard her mutter last weekend, when she was watching Summer sitting in her playpen, bashing the wooden sides with her favourite rattle and babbling nonsense to herself.

Gran says I could speak in sentences when I was Summer's age, but I don't think there's anything wrong with Summer at all. She just needs people to talk to her and then she will talk back.

"I'm just going to take Summer for a wee walk!" I call. Mum pokes her head round the kitchen door, and gives me a grateful smile. She looks shattered after her fight with Jenna. Her long, curly hair is all over the place and her eyes are red rimmed and tired.

"That's a great idea, Lily. She could do with some fresh air and it's a nice day. Thanks, love. Why don't you take some bread and feed the ducks?"

I squeeze past her, take a slice of rather stale brown bread from the bread bin and stuff it in the pocket of my hoodie.

I am hopeful that Mum will suggest I buy Summer an

ice cream, *And here's some money, Lily*, but sadly she doesn't. And asking Jenna for cash is a non-starter nowadays.

I bump the buggy down the two front steps and along the cracked little path to our gate. In two minutes we are whizzing down the High Street, past the newsagent's and the many gift shops and cafés, towards the pier. I slow down at the sweet shop.

"Look in there, Summer. Look at those yummy stripy lollipops and all those scrummy chocolates. I might get you a chocolate mouse next time. Would you like that?"

Summer makes some more of her garbled noises and sticks her hands up towards the sweet shop window. She stiffens, throws herself backwards in her pushchair and lets out a wail. I don't think she wants to wait until next time for a chocolate mouse. She wants one *right now*. Stopping here was a bad idea. I push the pram faster along the pavement.

We have to dodge past hordes of people on the narrow pavement, but I am quite good at using the buggy as a battering ram if they won't get out of the way.

"Whee! We're going to see the ducks, Summer! What do the ducks say? Quack, quack!"

I enjoy chatting to Summer as we go. She doesn't seem

to mind that I'm just havering, and she laughs and burbles gleefully.

The Cumbrae ferry is just about to leave and we stop at the pier to watch the cars, cyclists and foot passengers boarding. I smile because I'll be on it with Gran soon. Raucous seagulls wheel and swoop overhead, hoping to grab any discarded food. "Rats with wings," my mum calls them. She has a real thing about rodents.

One particularly cheeky seagull swoops down, big and grey and hungry. It launches itself at the queue of people and snatches a sandwich right out of a wee girl's outstretched hand.

"Sno' fair!" she wails. "That burd's nicked ma piece!"

"Did you see that, Summer?" I ask. "Did you see what the naughty birdie did?"

Summer grins at me, her baby teeth white in her grubby wee face, but I don't know if she understands what I'm saying.

Summer and I watch the foot passengers handing over their tickets and walking down the slope to the ferry. Many of them are pushing bikes. I wish I was going with them. When everyone's aboard, the big metal door rises and traps the cars inside. Most of the passengers head upstairs to enjoy the fresh sea breeze. I want to be up there too.

It's a warm, sunny afternoon and I'm too hot in my black hoodie and joggers. Summer looks fried. Her chubby cheeks are going bright pink so I unzip her anorak, trying to cool her down. I immediately wish I'd put a clean dress on her before we left. Her t-shirt is stained and grubby and her face is in dire need of a wash. Still, she's smiling cheerily and waving her toy lion at everyone she passes, and is clearly delighted to be outside.

"Look at the big boat, Summer!" I say, pointing at the ferry as it glides away from the pier and out into the firth. "It's going across the sea! Wave bye-bye!"

Summer waves enthusiastically at the ferry. I tell her that one day I'll take her on it and we'll go to Millport together.

Jenna would be making puking noises, but I don't care what Jenna thinks at the moment. I'm enjoying being out with my little sister. At least *she* doesn't think I'm a sanctimonious little creep and a goody two shoes. Summer thinks I'm the bee's knees.

"Let's go and see the ducks now. They will be getting hungry, won't they? Remember what the ducks say?"

I look at Summer expectantly, but she just grins, and waves her lion about madly. Maybe Gran's right about the developmental delay.

I push the buggy on to the promenade and walk past the big brash amusement arcade and the line of bleeping grabber machines where I won Summer's lion. The Italian flags outside Nardini's café are flapping in the sea breeze and people are sitting on the little terrace outside drinking coffee and enjoying their ice creams. I would love to stop there and have an enormous fudge sundae, but I am totally skint so that's out of the question. I wouldn't have minded a sugary doughnut from the wee stand on the prom either. My stomach is rumbling.

We carry on along the promenade, zigzagging past dog walkers and day-trippers. I am heading for the boating pond, near the RNLI lifeboat station. Summer loves to feed the ducks. I can feel the bread I had grabbed from the bread bin, all squashed and crumbly in my pocket.

"Lily!"

I jump, and whirl round, anxiously. No, no, no. The voice can't have followed me here. The voice doesn't happen outside my house. Despite the sunshine, a chill seeps into my bones. Goosebumps appear on my arms.

"Lily! I'm over here!"

Rowan is calling and waving at me from the sea wall.

I am hit by a wave of relief and embarrassment at having jumped out of my skin. Maybe it's me who has post-traumatic stress disorder and not Jenna. I'm tense, nervous, not sleeping well (that might be because Bronx snores) and I'm hearing voices. These are not good signs. I've googled all those symptoms on Jenna's laptop, which wasn't a great plan. It's too easy to convince yourself you are dying of some rare and ghastly disease. Plus, if Jenna catches me using her computer, she'll kill me. All in all, googling is not the healthy option.

Rowan Forrest has a sweet, round, freckled face with big, sparkly hazel eyes. Her brown curls are blowing in the wind and she's dressed in cute denim cut-offs and a bright yellow t-shirt. I feel suddenly self-conscious about my own lank, unwashed hair and old grey joggers. But she looks so smiley that I can't help smiling straight back. Rowan is the loveliest person in the world and it's a criminal offence to feel jealous of her.

"Hi Lily!" she calls again and I wheel the pushchair towards her, both of us grinning and waving as if we're reunited after years apart, instead of having seen each other on Friday at school.

"Wow, you're getting to be a big girl," she says, smiling at Summer, who gazes back a bit warily. "Hi Summer!"

Rowan has her dog with her, a big, soppy black Labrador who slaps my legs with his wagging tail as he tries to clamber into the pushchair beside Summer.

"Get down, Finn!" Rowan yells and tugs at his lead. Finn ignores her and Summer shrieks with laughter as he licks the dirt from her face. *This can't be hygienic*, I think, so I tug too until Finn concedes defeat.

Rowan and I walk together towards the boating pond, though I struggle to keep up with her as Finn drags her along the promenade.

"Finn, leave those people alone!" she yells at regular intervals. "Finn, don't eat that boy's ice cream! Finn, stop rolling in that mess!"

Walking a dog is exhausting. A baby in a pushchair is a lot less bother.

"Finn, slow down!" shouts Rowan, as Finn yanks at the lead and drags her towards the beach. "Oh, Finn, don't pee there! People sit on that wall!"

It's hard to have a proper conversation with Rowan when Finn's around. I change my mind about getting a dog of my own when I grow up. Maybe I will just stick with cats. They don't pee against walls.

The crowds of day-trippers thin as we move away from the ice-cream stands and noisy bumper cars on the front. This is my favourite part of the town. The Firth of Clyde is sparkling in the sunlight, with white-sailed yachts bobbing in the waves and seagulls wheeling in the clear blue sky. I love living by the sea, even in winter when wild, frothy waves crash over the sea wall and the sky is concrete grey.

"Look at the sea, Summer! It's all glittery!" I shout over the buzz of a jet ski.

Today you can see for miles. I can see Arran's hills in the distance and, much further away, humpbacked Ailsa Craig. The Isle of Cumbrae is only a mile across the water.

"I'm going to swim across to Cumbrae one day," I tell Rowan. "It looks easy, doesn't it?"

"You'd better wear a wet suit then," she laughs. "Or you'll get hypothermia and have to be rescued by the coastguard. Don't be fooled by its lovely blue colour – the water's freezing!"

At the boating pond, I let Summer out of the buggy and we feed the ducks with the crumbly remains of the stale slice of bread. Summer runs around the pond's edge, with Rowan and me chasing behind her.

"Quack, quack!" she burbles. "Look, look. Quack!"

See, Gran, I think triumphantly. She can speak when she has something to say.

Summer is so happy and excited about being out in the Big Wide World that I make her a silent promise that I will take her out more often. Maybe next time I will bring the boys as well. They could do with some fresh air.

"Doggie woof!" she shouts gleefully, and toddles over to give Finn a cuddle. "Ducks quack!" she yells, and spins round to walk towards the ducks in the pond. I can't believe she has been hiding so many words in her head all this time.

"Your wee sister is so cute, Lily," says Rowan. "I wish I had a baby sister. You're so lucky."

I feel a glow of pride, which lasts only until Summer trips over on a concrete paving stone and bangs her knee. She starts to wail and refuses to be comforted, making herself rigid in my arms and shrieking, tears spurting from her eyes and her nose running with snot.

I hurriedly stuff her, still howling, back into the pushchair and say that maybe I'd better get home.

Rowan kneels down in front of the pushchair, facing my screaming sister. I hope Summer doesn't aim a kick straight into her face. I can imagine what Rowan's mum would say about me if I went and let my sister give her a black eye.

"Summer, if you stop making that awful noise, I'll buy you an ice cream. Would you like that?" she says calmly.

The bribe works like magic. Summer might not say much, but she understands exactly what's being said to her. She stops crying, grins and pumps her arms up and down excitedly, waving her lion by its fluorescent-pink mane.

"Gimme!" she shouts. She seems to be getting more vocal by the minute. "Gimme ice cleam!"

So we walk back along the front a little way. I promise I'll pay Rowan back as she buys a cone for Summer and another for me. I try and coax a thank you from Summer before I hand over her cone, but she looks mutinous and I decide not to risk another screaming match.

We sit on the pebbly beach and I lick the melting ice cream as it drips down my hands. Finn chases seagulls and Summer sits happily stacking stones and then knocking them over. She is a sticky mess of ice cream, dirt and snot. Gran would have a fit if she saw her in this state.

"So, how's your weekend been?" I ask Rowan, keeping my voice light. I'm desperate to blurt out that I am being haunted by a ghostly voice and that today in the hall cupboard the voice had called me by name, but you can't really just come out with that kind of stuff can you?

For one thing, I know how concerned and upset she would be. She would want me to tell my mum. She would demand that I see a doctor. She would probably tell her mum too, and I already know how her mum feels about me and my family.

"Oh, great thanks," Rowan replies, as I knew she would. I have given the same answer to that question many times, but I have often been telling a lie. Rowan doesn't have to, she wouldn't even understand why you might want to lie about your feelings.

"Euan's home from uni for the holidays, but he says he is going to go backpacking all summer, so I won't see much of him, I don't think. Dad says he should stay home and get a summer job. What about you, Lily? Are you and Jenna going to Millport again?"

I stare across the water and try to imagine myself there, safe from ghostly voices and screeching sisters.

"I'm going with Gran in the last week of term," I tell her. "Jenna doesn't want to come this time."

"Oh no! Does that mean you'll miss the Leavers' Dance?" Rowan asks, frowning.

"Yeah, but you know I'm not that bothered about it," I say. 'Not that bothered' hardly covers how I feel about the ghastly prospect of a school dance… wearing a second-hand dress, dancing awkwardly in an overheated hall. Total nightmare. Rowan will be fine – she's got loads of other friends besides me and David.

"It won't be nearly as much fun without you there," she sighs. "So Jenna's not going on holiday, huh?" she adds, swiftly changing the subject. "Won't you be bored or lonely?"

"Nope," I reply. "I'm going to have the best time. Ever."

But as I speak, I realise with a start that there is someone else here, standing beside us on the pebbles and sand. I start to shiver, even though it's really warm. I can't see a ghostly figure or anything, but I can feel a shadow, as if a cloud has drifted across the sun. The voice whispers suddenly and insistently in my ear.

"Lily, did you say something?" it says. "Is that you, Lily?"

I shudder with shock and distress. The voice has followed me. I can't get away from it. I can feel my face crumpling and tears start to fall. Rowan hugs me, totally bewildered, as I begin to sob.

"What's wrong, Lily? Do you not want to go on holiday with your gran?" she asks anxiously. "Is it because you'll miss the dance? Please don't cry, Lil."

I shake my head.

"I *do* want to go to Millport. And I really don't care about missing the dance," I say in a trembling, muffled voice.

"Well, why are you crying? Please tell me. What's the matter, Lily?"

But how can I tell her what's wrong? How can I tell her that I'm being haunted?

I make a feeble excuse about having a headache, grab hold of Summer, fasten her into her pushchair and hurry home, afraid that if I tell my best friend the truth, she'll think I've gone crazy.

Chapter 4

Reasons I'm not happy today:

- ★ I am still being stalked by a disembodied voice.
- ★ I have to wear repulsive pink cast-offs that don't even fit properly, and have ruffles.
- ★ I worry a lot that my step-dad will come back.

When I finally get home, I am half blinded by tears and swelteringly hot from running while pushing a buggy. I fling the front door open, leave Summer asleep in her pushchair in the hall and run upstairs.

Mum is in her bedroom, brushing her hair, getting ready for her Sunday evening shift at the café. I enter before I have time to talk myself out of it.

"Mum, I'm scared," I blurt out. But then I can't think what to say next. I'm really afraid that she'll think I'm going mad. *I* already think I'm going mad.

Mum looks really upset when she sees me. I catch sight of myself in the mirror propped on the chest of drawers and I can see why. My face, which can't have been one hundred per cent clean, is streaked with tears. My eyes are red and swollen and my hair is damp with sweat. There are dribbles of ice cream down my front. I am not a pretty sight.

"Come here, sweetheart," says Mum. "Come and tell me what's wrong."

Mum draws me towards her and we sit together on the bed. Mum's bed is unmade and strewn with her clothes. She likes to wear long, floaty cotton skirts with black leggings and *lots* of scarves. She thinks she looks romantic but sometimes she just looks odd.

Summer's cot, an untidy jumble of soft toys and blankets, stands in one corner of the room and a huge old-fashioned wardrobe stands against the wall. There is hardly room to move.

"I'm just scared," I say pathetically, cuddling up to her as if I was Summer.

"It's ok, Lily, I understand," Mum says quietly, arm tight round my shoulders. "It was a scary, upsetting time and of course you're not over it yet. But he's gone, I promise you."

She's talking about my step-dad. She thinks I'm afraid he'll come back. I suppose that does worry me sometimes, but he isn't my main problem at the moment, not by a mile.

"Your step-father isn't allowed to come within a five mile radius of Largs, Lily. We will never see him again. I'm just so, so sorry I brought him into your lives in the first place."

I'm sorry she ever met him, and sometimes I'm angry too. It was a bad five years, and five years is nearly half of my life. Living with an alcoholic is a horrible thing that I wouldn't wish on my worst enemy. (Not that I have a worst enemy. I avoid conflict at all costs, and will always apologise first, even when it clearly isn't my fault. Basically, I'm the world's biggest wimp.)

Anyway, back to the part I didn't really want to talk about.

My step-dad was unpredictable. Sometimes he would just drink himself into a stupor and fall asleep, snoring and ugly, on the couch. But other times, completely without warning, he would fly into violent, terrifying drunken rages. He would jerk around like an out-of-control robot, limbs flailing and voice thick and slurred. Ornaments would smash, plates would get thrown, ugly words spat at whoever got in his way. Personally I think Mum should have flung him out long, long before she did.

It was the worst, scariest, saddest night of all, the night

Mum called the police and they came and arrested my step-dad. Mum was in hysterics, Jenna was screaming blue murder, I was sobbing and terrified. But it was also one of the best nights I can remember. After all the drama was over, we all piled, tearful and shattered, into Mum's bed and snuggled under her duvet with mugs of hot chocolate while she cuddled us tight and told us he would never be back. Jenna and I had avoided Mum's bedroom for five years, because that was his territory. It felt so lovely to be back.

And we all lived happily ever after.

Well, not quite; this isn't a fairy story. But when he'd gone, we could breathe freely again. Sure, we had to move into a smaller, rented house, which can be a nightmare, and we are always short of money, but the joys of breathing freely should not be underestimated.

"You know Lily, I don't say thanks to you often enough. You are such a big help to me and the wee ones and you never complain. What would we all do without our Lil?" asks Mum. There are tears in her eyes.

I sit there with my mum, enjoying the hug, and not wanting to spoil things by telling the truth. And the truth is that this isn't about my step-dad. This is new. Still scary, but much weirder. I am crying because the voice followed me out of the house and down to the seafront. I am afraid that I will never be free of the voice and I will never breathe freely again.

The doorbell rings and Mum jumps up, wipes her eyes and goes downstairs to answer it. I hear her opening the front door and then closing it quietly behind her. She has gone outside to talk privately to whoever is there. I guess that it's Gran and that Mum is outside now explaining that Jenna doesn't want to come on holiday to Millport with her this year. I'm pretty sure that won't go down well.

Sure enough, I hear my gran's loud, strident voice and bury my head under Mum's duvet. I don't feel up to coping with Gran, especially if she's on the rampage.

"Lily!" she yells. "Jenna! Come here, girls, please!"

I run upstairs to the bathroom and give my face a quick wash. I stick my tongue out at my red-eyed reflection and remind myself that I am a strong person. Rowan is always telling me that. It's one of the reasons I love her so much. She is completely honest and always says what she feels, like Anne of Green Gables, and unlike me. If Rowan tells you something about yourself, you're sure it must be true.

"Lily!" shouts my gran. "Come when you're called!"

I amble casually through to the living room, where Gran is standing, the image of a cartoon battleaxe, face grim and arms folded round her large chest, glaring at the clothes draped over the chairs and at the toys scattered on the carpet. Bronx and Hudson sit awestruck on the couch, silent for the first time today. Thank goodness they're dressed at least. Gran is a frightening sight when she is preparing for battle.

"You girls should be more help to your mother," she snaps, as Jenna slouches in behind me. "Look at the state of this place. It's a disgrace!"

Mum flushes crimson but says nothing.

I pick up a small jumper and fold it neatly, then run over and hug my gran around her ample middle.

"I am so excited about going to Millport, Gran!" I say, with rather sickly enthusiasm. Sure enough, when I turn around, Jenna is sticking her fingers down her throat and pretending to vomit.

"You'll need a swimming costume and some decent summer clothes," says Gran, looking disparagingly at my grey joggers and hoodie. "You can't come with me looking like that."

"She looks fine to me," blurts Mum, and Jenna snorts rudely.

"She really doesn't, Mum," she says witheringly.

You can all stop talking about me now, I think fiercely, but say nothing as usual.

"Doesn't the child have *clean* clothes to wear, at least?" asks Gran, turning on Mum.

"Of course she does," replies Mum, which is an

absolutely made-up fiction. Virtually every bit of clothing I own is in the dirty laundry bin.

The growing tension between Mum and Gran is making me a bit anxious. What's wrong with me today? I'm not usually such a drip. I think Mum realises, because she puts her hand on my shoulder and squeezes gently.

"Lily can wear that lovely pink swimming costume… the one you bought for Jenna a couple of years ago. Jenna's grown out of it now. And we've already arranged a shopping trip to buy more summer clothes, haven't we, Lily? We're getting the train into Glasgow next Saturday," she adds.

This is all news to me, but I nod and smile in agreement, pleased at the thought of a trip into town with Mum. But inwardly I'm groaning at the thought of yet another of Jenna's pink cast-offs. I'm sure that awful swimsuit has ruffles too.

Jenna looks outraged that Mum and I have planned a shopping trip without her, but she can hardly complain that she isn't being included in a trip to buy clothes for a holiday on which she is refusing to come.

I smile innocently at her and she glares back icily. If looks could kill, I'd be on a mortuary slab.

Gran nods and smiles and I know she's just getting started. She starts to unbutton her beige raincoat. My gran always wears a coat, even on the warmest of days.

"That's great, Claire. I would like to help pay for the clothes, as I want Lily to look really smart on this holiday."

Gran says this while looking me up and down in a way that suggests I look the exact opposite of smart at the moment. I can feel my face blushing fiery red as Jenna grins meanly.

"And Jenna can babysit for the wee ones when you go into Glasgow," Gran adds spitefully. "I've got a coffee morning at my church next Saturday."

"But I've got plans for Saturday," Jenna yammers, the grin on her face dissolving instantly. "Jess and I are going—"

"You'll need to cancel your plans. You're babysitting," snaps Gran.

Gran dumps her shiny handbag on the floor and plonks her big behind down on the couch between a startled Bronx and Hudson, who have to leap out the way to avoid being squashed.

"Make me a cup of tea, Jenna," she barks. "Lily and I have our holiday plans to discuss. And I'd like a chocolate biscuit with my tea."

Jenna flounces out, looking torn between fury and relief at having to leave the room. She must have been worried that Gran would drag her unwillingly to Millport or roar at her for being an ungrateful brat. But Gran seems relatively resigned. Maybe she is secretly relieved, like I am.

"You need a bath and hair wash, madam," says Gran to me firmly. "A lady's hair is her crowning glory, you know."

She turns to Mum and shoos her, as if she were an annoying insect.

"Off you go to work, Claire. I'll take over here. And why are you letting the baby sleep at this time of day, for heaven's sake?"

Five minutes later, Mum leaves for work, her eyes flashing with annoyance and her mouth full of bitter words which will spill out later when Gran isn't around.

As soon as Mum has slammed the door behind her, Gran sets us all to work. Sunday evening is its usual whirl of tidying, cleaning and washing. I don't complain. In fact I relish those Sunday nights. They restore some order to our lives and ensure that, at least on a Monday morning, we all look clean and respectable.

"You girls need to help your mother more," Gran complains repeatedly, and while Jenna stuffs her fingers in her ears, I'm listening guiltily.

It's not that I don't want to be helpful. I know Mum is tired when she gets home from cleaning other people's houses. I know she needs help to keep this house looking nice. It's just that housework is so dull and repetitive. You can spend ages making a room all tidy, clean and vacuumed and then a few minutes later Bronx and Hudson will have scattered action figures, lego blocks and biscuit crumbs over every surface. All your hard work is ruined and you are back to square one.

Sometimes – ok, most of the time – I'd rather read a book or listen to the radio. But on Sunday nights, I'm happy to put in the effort and even Jenna, who usually grudges every moment spent away from her precious laptop, scrubs the kitchen floor and washes down the tiles in the bathroom without an excessive amount of moaning.

"Well done, girls," says Gran, when we collapse in a heap on the couch. She is bashing our clothes into submission with an iron, thumping it against the board as she turns tangled heaps of laundry into neat, organised piles.

"Now, doesn't it feel good knowing you'll be nice and smart for school tomorrow?" she asks nobody in particular. "Go and pack your bags and lay out your uniforms. Lily, you get Bronx organised for the morning."

Gran runs a bath for us all using some of Mum's Christmas bubble bath. Jenna gets the water first because she is oldest and grumpiest. I am bitterly jealous of all the frothy, fluffy mango-scented bubbles. It looks bliss.

"Get out of here," snarls Jenna, pushing past me into the bathroom and shoving me towards the door. "Give me peace."

I wonder if she and I will ever be friends again, or if we will be at each other's throats forever. I miss the big sister I had before she metamorphosed into a monster. Even if she was a werewolf like the ones in her stupid vampire books, then at least she would be normal for most of the time, and we'd only live in terror of her when there was a full moon.

"Lily, get in that bath and give yourself a good scrub!" yells Gran, ten minutes later.

The water is a bit lukewarm and scummy with shampoo and soap by the time I get in. But lying back in the deep water is peaceful and relaxing. Gran has brought some coconut shampoo from her own house and I use it to wash my hair. When it's washed and blow-dried, my wispy gingery hair will look all glossy, light and fluffy. I will be able to toss it carelessly from side to side like those daft girls in the shampoo adverts.

Eventually, I drag myself out of the bath, dry myself on a damp towel and look in the bathroom mirror. That's better. My face is flushed and pink and I look almost pretty, though my nose is still too long and my face is thin and pointy. My eyes are an odd, light-grey colour, like beach pebbles.

"Lily?" says the voice, right into my ear. "Is that you, Lily?"

I whirl around, trying to catch the voice in the act. I think I catch a glimpse of a vague, shadowy outline of a person, but can't be sure.

"Who are you?" I whisper. But nobody answers. The only sounds are the dripping tap and the distant whirring of the washing machine.

Chapter 5

Reasons not to get involved in school sports:

⭐ I haven't got a competitive bone in my body.
⭐ Being all hot and sweaty doesn't appeal
   when there may be no clean shirts in
   the house until Gran sorts stuff at
   the weekend.
⭐ I'm always one of the last to get chosen
   when they pick teams in gym lessons (unless
   Rowan is doing the picking). Why would I
   want more of that in my own time?

When I meet Rowan and David at the school gate on
Monday morning, I can tell they've been plotting. David
smiles at me and I know by his look that Rowan has told
him I was upset on the beach yesterday. He is sorry for

me, and there is nothing I hate more than being pitied. Rowan's brown curls are tied back in a red ribbon and she is neat and pretty in the same school uniform that makes me look like a World War Two evacuee.

"Hi Lily," she says cheerfully. "Are you feeling better?"

"I'm fine thanks," I reply. 'Fine' is one of my most overused words. I hide the truth with 'fine' all the time. "So, another week in the hellhole," I say cheerfully, as I let go of Bronx's hand and let him loose to run wild in the playground. Hudson has already bounded ahead, having sighted his friends from afar. "I can't believe the weekend's over already."

Rowan and David both know that I'm havering. I love school. My keenness to be involved in nearly all things school-related is legendary. No wonder Jenna thinks I'm a creep. My jobs at school include being on the pupil council and eco committee, running the Fairtrade shop, litter picking, being a lunch buddy to the wee ones and a wet play monitor when it rains. The only thing I draw the line at is sport. Yes, I would rather pick up empty juice cartons and half-eaten sandwiches than be hit in the face by a netball any day. Rowan plays after-school netball and badminton but I refuse point blank to get involved.

"David and I have a plan," says Rowan, grabbing my arm and grinning. She clearly can't wait to tell me about it.

"School breaks up at twelve o'clock on Friday the 26th June. Yes?"

"Yes. Great work, Sherlock," I say.

"You'll still be in Millport. So, David and I are going to talk our parents into spending Friday afternoon on Cumbrae. We can all meet up at the Garrison, have a picnic and cycle round the island. It will be great!"

David nods his head in such enthusiastic agreement that his NHS wire glasses slide from his nose, and he has to push them back on, blinking furiously. "We can bring a picnic, or maybe get lunch in the Fintry Bay café," he says, his face crinkling with the effort of making such a big decision.

David is like a miniature mad professor, with his wild sticky-out hair, round glasses and permanent worried frown. He has been our friend since Primary 3, which was the year he realised that he was never going to fit in with the boys in the class. David hates football and has no interest at all in video games. Back then, all he wanted to talk about was dinosaurs. Now it's Star Wars.

"I think definitely a picnic. We can bring a rug and have it on the beach. With lashings of ginger beer!" giggles Rowan. "It'll be like the *Famous Five*."

"Yeah, except there's only three of us," I smile back. "I don't want my gran and your dog coming along to make five. Finn would snaffle all the picnic and my gran would nag for Scotland about our table manners."

David shudders – whether at the thought of the dog

(he's allergic) or my gran's nagging, I'm not sure.

"Enid Blyton stories are full of negative gender stereotypes," he says pompously. I expect he got that from his mum. She is always coming out with that sort of thing.

"But George in the *Famous Five* was a fantastic role model for girls," replies Rowan coolly, "back when we were all expected to be good little housekeepers."

Rowan always has a smart answer. Not sarky; genuinely smart. Just then the school bell rings and saves David from having to discuss a subject he is clueless about.

We run to get into the long straggling line of other Primary 7s. All the boys look tall and skinny next to wee David and they ignore him when he joins the line. They think he's weird, and aren't always very kind to him, but David isn't that bothered. He says all the other boys in the class are Neanderthals or neds, or both.

My hair feels as light and bouncy as I'd hoped and my uniform is clean and crisp. I feel good about myself for a change, and secretly thrilled that Rowan and David are going to join me at the end of my holiday. And I love that neither of them has freaked about me going away on the last week of term – maybe because we all know we'll be at high school together anyway. They are my best friends in the world, and I don't ever want to lose them. There are plenty of girls in the class who would steal Rowan from me if they could.

"Hi Rowan!" shouts Georgia, her friend from the netball club. "You should see the dress Jade's bought to wear to the Leavers' Dance!"

"Come round after school and have a look," twitters Jade. "See what you think."

"It's stunning!" shrieks Georgia. "You two are going to look gorgeous and I'm going to look a complete state."

I sigh. Somebody compliment her quickly, or she'll shrivel up and die. Rowan and Jade oblige and tell her she is going to look totally beautiful. Her dress is blue satin with spaghetti straps, in case you're interested. No, me neither.

Georgia and Jade move up so that Rowan can slip into line next to them. She starts giggling and tossing her hair about and I get nervous. "Don't do that, Rowan," I murmur to myself, "it looks dumb and you are a zillion miles from dumb."

I'm on my own waiting in line for Mrs McKenzie, and as always when I'm alone, my anxiety about the voice creeps up on me. Why won't the voice leave me alone? All it's doing is asking stupid questions. It doesn't even seem sure about what it's saying half the time. Either I'm being haunted by the world's dumbest ghost or I'm going senile, like old Mrs Simpson at number 45, who thinks aliens are hiding in her dustbin.

"Lily, hurry up!" calls David. "You're holding up the line!"

I don't know why I keep calling the voice 'it' when I

know it's a girl. Who could she possibly be? She sounds familiar but the only dead people who might be interested in haunting me are my dad and my grandfather and it's certainly not one of them.

"Lily McLean, do you intend to stand out in the playground all morning?" snaps Mrs McKenzie. "Hurry up and get into class!"

I walk in, still thinking about Dad and Grandpa Jim. Not that I can really remember either of them, and certainly not what they sounded like.

Sometimes I take Mum's old photo album down from the shelf, brush off the dust, stare at the photos of my dad and try and conjure up some memories, but I can't. In one of the photos he's holding Jenna's hand and carrying me in a kind of backpack. He's tall and thin, with fair, receding hair and he is grinning at whoever is taking the photograph. I have wispy hair and a chubby face and I'm scowling. I expect I was hungry. We are on a mountain and it's a gloriously sunny day.

Mum says Dad loved hill climbing. He was mad keen on it, along with cycling and water sports – a real fresh air and fitness freak, unlike me. He died in a car accident when I was two, which wasn't fair on any of us, especially poor Dad.

Anyway, it isn't a man who is whispering in my ear, which is a tiny bit of a relief. That would certainly up the freaky factor.

As Mrs McKenzie takes the register, I relax into the structure and routine of the school day. It's what I most love about school. It might be dull, but it's predictable. When things were really awful at home, when my step-dad was at his worst, this school was my safe place. (Our old house in Kelvin Street didn't have a hall cupboard.)

"Lily McLean, are you listening to a word I say?"

I jump as Mrs McKenzie looms suddenly over my desk.

"I was telling the rest of the class about our school trip to Vikingar! We are going in the last week of term. Isn't that exciting? Please return your permission slip ASAP, Lily."

She looks at me rather pointedly. Mum is not good at getting round to filling in permission slips, but I am becomingly reasonably expert at doing them myself. Not that there's much point in filling in this one. I'll be in Millport. I remember to pull out a crumpled envelope from my school bag and hand it to Mrs McKenzie. She eyes it suspiciously. I wrote it myself last night so I know exactly what it says.

Dear Mrs McKenzie,

Please excuse Lily's absence in the last week of term (22-26 June.) She is travelling to the Isle of Cumbrae with her grandmother, who is very unwell and has made a last request to have a

short break on the island. Lily's gran has very
little time left and so we have arranged for
Lily to spend some quality time with her. I hope
this will not cause too much inconvenience. She
will catch up on any missed work.

Yours sincerely,
Claire McLean

I am hoping they believe my letter and give me an authorised absence. Unauthorised absences look bad on my record, and I don't like to look bad. I'd much rather tell a whopping lie. And the added benefit is that next year I will be in secondary school, so this particular lie is reusable.

Mrs McKenzie hands the letter back to me. Her penetrating look tells me that she knows perfectly well that I am a liar and a forger of notes.

"Your mother's handwriting is so remarkably like your own, Lily," she says sharply. "Take the letter along to the office, please. I'm sorry about your gran's illness. She seemed very far from frail when she came up to the school for parent's evening. And it's a real shame that you're going to miss the trip, the Leavers' Dance and the school service."

I feel my face redden and almost snatch the letter out of Mrs McKenzie's outstretched hand. As I walk along to the school office, I try to work out my feelings. I am really gutted about missing the trip to Vikingar!

My feelings towards missing the Leavers' Dance haven't changed though. The girls at school have been going on for weeks about prom dresses and haircuts and nail varnish and make-up and sharing limos. Even Rowan's been caught up in the drama, much to my and David's shared annoyance.

Rowan's mum has announced, however, that the whole limo thing is ridiculous and out of the question. Rowan will have to walk up to school like a regular mortal on the night of the dance. Georgia, whose dad is forking out for the limo, will be furious, and Rowan thinks it'll be the end of the world when she tells her. But I'm pretty sure they'll live… it's hard to take those sorts of dramas seriously, and it sometimes makes me feel a bit weird and disconnected from the other girls, even from Rowan.

Anyway, I had been totally dreading the whole Leavers' Dance horror and I know David has too. He will be feeling a lot worse now that he knows I'm not going with him. We had planned to walk up to the school together, when we still thought Rowan was going to be riding there in style with the netball girls.

David's mum is hiring him a kilt from Murdo's and he says he looks like a total wally in it. I can sympathise completely. I specialise in looking a total wally. I've lost count of the times I have looked in the mirror and shuddered at the sight of me dressed in Jenna's cast-offs. Most of her old outfits are pink, which you'd never believe looking at her now, and it's not a colour which goes well with ginger hair like mine.

So of course the prom dress lined up for me was a pale pink, flouncy, net tutu confection that Jenna wore for her own leavers' dance. *She* looked gorgeous in it, like a little blonde fairy. *I* looked the exact opposite of that when I tried it on, and that's not me doing a Georgia and fishing for compliments. When I came out of the bedroom wearing it, Jenna roared with laughter. "Look, boys!" she shrieked. "A wee ginger fairy! Oh, Lily, that's hideous!"

"Don't be so mean, Jenna!" snapped Mum, but she looked worried, and later she suggested we dye the whole outfit blue.

Nothing whatsoever was said about buying me a new dress.

So, no, I'm still not sorry to be missing my primary school Leavers' Dance.

I wander back from the school office and find everyone changing for P.E. I'd forgotten today was a gym day. If I'd only remembered, I could have forged another note.

Please excuse Lily from P.E. Her leg was badly mauled by a lion during a trip to the zoo at the weekend.

Or

Please excuse Lily from P.E. Unfortunately, she has developed a serious allergy to forward rolls.

Or

Please excuse Lily from P.E. We have recently joined a small religious cult, which expressly forbids members from taking part in any form of organised physical exercise.

I like that one. It sounds the most believable. But I'm too late.

"Hurry up, Lily," snaps Mrs McKenzie.

I don't think Mrs McKenzie enjoys P.E. lessons any more than I do. Doug the Thug is a danger to himself and others in the gym hall. He wields a hockey stick like it's a machete.

Reluctantly, I change into my grimy t-shirt and too-tight

pink shorts and follow the rest of the class as they surge into the hall. Oh, great. It's netball. Plenty of opportunity for Doug to charge around the hall like a stampeding bull elephant. Lots of occasions for Georgia to elbow me surreptitiously in the ribs.

"Lily, could you fetch a ball please?"

No problem, Mrs McKenzie; anything to avoid the team-picking nightmare, even the messy gym-equipment store cupboard

I should have known the ghost would be in there. She clearly likes cupboards.

I'm rummaging about in the cluttered semi-darkness for a ball that isn't burst, or rugby- or tennis-ball shaped, when she speaks, right in my ear.

"Lily, if that is really you – listen to me – *don't go to Millport.*"

Panicked, I leap in the air, and dislodge an enormous stack of plastic hula-hoops. They cascade in a colossal clatter, bouncing, spinning and rolling around the floor. Mrs McKenzie rushes into the cupboard.

"What on earth has happened in here? Are you alright, Lily?"

"I feel a bit dizzy," I reply, truthfully. "Some of the hoops bounced off my head."

Mrs McKenzie sighs.

"You'd better pop along to the medical room and get

an ice pack. And then come back here and clear up all this mess."

I'm not dizzy from the hoops though, I'm dizzy because the voice was so insistent this time. She wasn't asking dumb questions, she was bossing me about. Did I hear her right? Why on earth wouldn't she want me to go to Millport?

By the time I've finished lying to the nurse about my near-fatal skull injury, and reordering the gym cupboard one-handed whilst holding an ice pack to my head – hoping the voice wouldn't speak again – Mrs McKenzie is blowing the final whistle. I've missed my last ever primary school P.E. lesson.

So being haunted isn't a total disaster.

Chapter 6

The most awful things that can happen on a train:

- ⭐ Hurtling past the platform and smashing into the ticket office.
- ⭐ Seeing a drunk jaikie, and realising he's a relation.
- ⭐ Getting 'the talk' from your mum in a packed carriage.

"Get up and get dressed, Lily. We're going shopping!" shouts Mum and I fling myself out of bed.

It's early on Saturday morning and Mum has kept her promise to buy me some new clothes.

"I'm coming, Mum!" I call, anxious not to wind her up before we've even left the house. I fling on my only clean clothes: a denim skirt that used to belong to Jenna and my favourite black hoodie.

It's a rare day that Jenna and I are both in a good mood, and today is one of them. She has been bribed to babysit with a promise of £10 to go with her friends to see the new vampire movie. And I am uber-excited at the prospect of a day out in the city with the added bonus of some time alone with Mum.

"You look nice, dear," she says, as we walk along to the station together.

"So do you, Mum," I reply, and for once I'm serious. Mum's wild curly hair is tied back in a ponytail with a pretty green scarf and her skirt is a matching dark green silk. She looks quite respectable. She is even wearing almost-ordinary shoes, instead of those horrible spiky-heeled suede boots she usually wears, which make her look as if she is dressing up as a witch for Halloween.

Largs station is right in the middle of the town. It's a relatively new station because twenty years ago a train failed to stop and hurtled right into the ticket office, crashed through the front of the station and ploughed into two shops, demolishing them. The train ended up at the taxi rank on Main Street. Gran says it's a miracle nobody was killed. Every time I stand on this platform, I imagine that the train won't stop again.

"This is lovely, isn't it, Lil?" says Mum happily. "It's so nice to have a wee day out, just the two of us."

I sit opposite Mum on the train as it speeds through the Ayrshire countryside, wondering if I should perhaps mention to her that almost every day this week a voice has whispered urgently in my ear. And that more recently it's been pretty clear that it thinks I shouldn't go on holiday. But I've got the same problem I had with telling Rowan. Mum will either think I've lost the plot completely or that I'm coming up with a particularly silly excuse not to go away with Gran.

"Which shops do you want to go to first?" asks Mum cheerfully. Gran has given her money to buy me clothes, so Mum doesn't have that strained, this-is-costing-me-more-than-I-can-afford look she often has when she is out shopping for us.

I shrug and say I don't mind. I really don't.

"You're very quiet these days, Lily," says Mum thoughtfully. She leans forward and takes my hand in hers. I snatch it back.

Not here, Mum, I think.

"Is there anything worrying you? You know the kind of thing… growing up, body changes? Do you have any questions you want to ask me?"

I turn crimson with embarrassment. Could she not have discussed these things when we were in the privacy of her bedroom last weekend? Not here, on a train crowded with Saturday shoppers.

"Mum, we're on the train," I groan, hoping nobody has heard us. "Please don't talk about that stuff *now*."

"It's important stuff, Lily," says Mum. "You're at an age when you need as much reliable information as possible. You mustn't feel embarrassed. You can ask your old mum anything."

I am in a positive agony of embarrassment by now. My face is on fire. My whole body is burning.

"I've had the talk from the nurse at school, Mum," I hiss, through clenched teeth. "Can we do this another time, please?"

By now I'm certain that every passenger in the carriage is craning their necks to catch every word. Mum must feel she has humiliated me enough, because she doesn't say any more about it. Just as well, because if this train had a trapdoor in the floor I would risk death to clamber out on to the railway line.

Mum picks up a *Metro* newspaper from the train seat and starts to read the headlines aloud to me instead.

"Listen to this, Lily! A burglar was caught after he dropped his mobile phone on the floor of the house he was robbing. Pretty stupid, eh?" she trills.

"Hmm," I murmur, wishing she would just stop talking.

Mum thrusts the paper towards me to show me a photograph of a famous soap star. He is standing outside a courthouse, arms raised in celebration after being cleared of drug dealing.

"He looks totally guilty to me," she says gleefully. "Look at those shifty eyes."

I pretend I don't know her and look steadily out of the grimy window as the landscape changes from rural to urban. We cross the River Clyde and I stare out at the bridges, tall office buildings and the fancy flats lining the riverside. Soon the train is sliding into Glasgow Central and we are spilling out of it on to the platform.

"Right! Primark first I think!" shouts Mum, over the din of the crowds and the traffic. As we stroll up Buchanan Street, we listen to guitar-strumming buskers and laugh at some street theatre guys who loom over us on enormous stilts. I always enjoy Glasgow's buzz, but I would never want to live so far from the sea.

We head up to Sauchiehall Street and then the Buchanan Galleries. Mum even lets me browse for nearly half an hour in the bookshop while she leafs through home decoration magazines she has no intention of buying.

The shopping expedition goes reasonably well. Mum and I hardly fight at all over my clothes choices, though I get pretty hacked off when she puts her foot down in Topshop.

"I like them," I say defiantly, holding up a pair of purple leather shorts. Short shorts. "They're a lovely colour. I'd wear them all the time."

"That's what I'm afraid of, Lily," sighs Mum. "I'm sure

they would look ok on a girl of Jenna's age, but they are completely inappropriate for a wee girl like you."

I bristle about being called a wee girl, but I guess maybe Gran won't like the shorts either, and it is her money we're spending, so I back down and choose denim ones instead.

In a very short time Gran's money is almost gone. I have three new t-shirts, skinny jeans, two pairs of denim shorts and a pair of canvas shoes, which I particularly love, because they are neon orange and have multi-coloured laces. I like bright colours. Jenna says I have no taste.

Plus Mum buys some new knickers for me, and my first ever bra, but I'm not prepared to discuss *that* humiliation. Mum even insisted on asking the girl in the shop to measure my bra size. My face is still such a bright scarlet that I'm clashing with my new orange shoes.

If I had known she was planning to kit me out for womanhood, I would never have come on this expedition. I thought I was just here to get summer clothes. I feel tricked.

But also, I have to admit, a bit relieved. Bra ownership isn't really a major issue for me at the moment, as I have no boobs whatsoever, but I definitely don't want to start secondary school wearing my age 9–11 vest and pants.

After the considerable trauma of the bra, I'm glad to sit in the coffee shop at the station with Mum. She is nursing a cinnamon latte bought with the rest of Gran's money, while I sip on a coke, munch on a blueberry muffin and write in the gorgeous new red leather journal I bought with the tenner Gran slipped me last Sunday. Good old Gran.

I am engrossed in my list-making when I get the strange feeling that I'm being watched. I swivel my eyes to the left, pretending that I'm still busy writing. There is someone sitting in the chair beside me. I can see the outline of a girl, but she's so grey and insubstantial that I know if I put my hand out I will touch air. She's just a faint, almost featureless outline, like a shimmering bubble. This must be her – the ghost, the voice – visible at last. Well, almost visible.

Slowly and creepily, she leans towards me, her long hair swinging, and she says something, but there's too much background noise and I can't make out what she's saying. I turn my head towards her and look right into her eyes, so dark and grey that they seem at first to be empty sockets. Her features are so fuzzy that I can't even tell if she is happy or sad.

"Lily. It is you, isn't it? Can you see me too?" she whispers. "Don't go away—"

"Are you ok, Lily?" says Mum, with a worried frown. The girl fades into nothingness like a wisp of smoke. "You're very pale."

"I'm fine, Mum. I just felt a bit dizzy for a moment," I reply, feeling decidedly spooked and shaky. Did the girl mean don't go away *now* or don't go *away*, like to Millport? She isn't making herself very clear, in more ways than one.

"Oh dear, we'd better get you home," says Mum, standing up and gathering the carrier bags. "The train leaves in five minutes."

We rush to the platform and climb aboard the Largs train. I lean my head against the cold glass and close my eyes. This is too much, it really is. I need to tell somebody I'm seeing ghosts. I'll be like the wee boy in that *ParaNorman* movie: 'I can see dead people.'

No, there's no way I am saying that out loud.

There's a loud whistle and the train pulls out of the station.

Mum is chatting away to me when she suddenly gasps and goes silent mid-sentence. I open my eyes and squeeze them shut again. I don't want to see what is looming in front of us. I would rather have faced my ghost girl again.

My step-dad is lurching along the aisle between the rows of seats. He is looking for a seat, but he's clearly drunk and people are placing their bags on the empty seats next to them. Nobody wants a drunk jaikie sitting near them.

"'Scuse me, 'scuse me," he slurs, as he nearly falls into somebody's lap.

He hasn't seen Mum yet and if we're careful, I think that we might escape unnoticed. Mum grabs my hand and hisses at me to get my journal out of the carrier bag on the floor. I bend down to fetch it and she leans down at the same time, pretending to rummage in our bags.

My step-dad sways forward and flings himself clumsily into a seat just three rows from us. The face of the elderly lady directly opposite him is a mask of distaste. He is half lying across the train seat, feet sticking out in the aisle. He looks scruffy and unwashed and I expect he smells pretty unpleasant.

"Just sit quietly and write in your journal," whispers Mum. "He'll never know we're on the train as long as we don't draw attention to ourselves."

Mum winds her scarf round her head, covering her hair and part of her face, and then leans her head against the window and closes her eyes. I stare down at my journal as if I'm concentrating really hard, but the words are jumping about on the page. My heart is jumping about in my ribcage too. And my hands are shaking too much to write.

The train carries on rumbling along the rails and I pray silently that he won't turn around.

I'm not sure exactly who I'm praying to, as I stopped believing in God when I was in Primary 4 and our teacher told us the story of Noah. I didn't want to believe in a God who would decide to kill everyone in the whole world, except one family, because the majority of people weren't behaving very nicely. He sent masses of rain and flooded the land, and all those bad people drowned. I've read that drowning is one of the worst ways to go, so that makes it even more cruel. My family wouldn't have made it on to the Ark, that's for sure. We would have drowned with the rest of the bad guys.

The train whizzes through the countryside, stopping regularly at the small stations on the line. As we stop at Johnstone, Milliken Park and then Howwood, I wonder uneasily when my step-dad is going to get off the train.

Mum has told me many times that he isn't allowed to come within a five-mile radius of Largs. I picture miles and miles of jagged barbed-wire fence, probably electrified. And a wide circle of armed guards holding the collars of snarling, slavering dogs. I imagine these things because they make me feel safe, even though I know they are silly, and that in real life the only thing preventing my step-dad from turning up at our front door is the legal injunction organised by McTavish and Quipp (the lawyers, obviously, not the cats).

So he can't be getting off at our station, surely. I begin to feel quite panicky at the thought of him staying on the train all the way to Largs. What if he follows us home?

"Mum, when's he going to get off?" I whisper, hearing the anxiety in my voice.

"Next station, I expect, Lily," says Mum confidently. "He is staying with his mother and she lives out this way."

The train slows with a screeching of brakes as we

approach Glengarnock. My step-dad heaves himself to his feet and staggers towards the doors and it's as he stands, clutching the rail, waiting for the doors to slide open, that I notice how much weight he has lost. How yellow and papery his skin looks.

He almost falls out of the train and reels towards the station exit. Mum gives me a shaky smile, but her eyes look desperately sad and I feel the same. For the first time since my step-dad came into my life, I feel sorry for him, and not nearly so afraid. He looked pathetic; not the bogeyman I remember. Not that I am sorry to see the back of him. Hopefully I will never have to see him again as long as I live.

The train rumbles on towards Largs, and when I catch sight of the Firth of Clyde glistening in the June sunshine, my heart lifts. We're home! And with any luck, I've left the ghostly girl behind in Glasgow.

"Come on Lil!" smiles Mum, gathering up the bags. "Let's head home and show everyone what we've bought."

"Not *everything* we've bought, Mum," I say quickly, snatching the bag containing the bra out of her hand, before she reveals it to the world.

Chapter 7

Things I will miss about primary school:

* Golden Time on Friday afternoons. I don't think they do that at high school so much.
* Library duty with the little ones.
* Surprisingly, Mrs McKenzie.

The next week drags horribly. Mum lends me her fake Gucci holdall for my holiday clothes and I spend quite a lot of time packing and repacking. I decide not to write any more in my new journal until I'm in Millport and so I pack it along with a new pen, my wee radio, and all my new clothes. Jenna is being almost nice to me. She offered me her not-too-old cardigan for a start, mumbling something about keeping me warm, and she hasn't had another meltdown since last Sunday's spectacular.

"It'll be weird without you mooning around the house," she says to me on Tuesday as we trail over to Gran's to collect a chicken casserole. Gran often cooks us meals to be put in our freezer and defrosted in a food emergency. There are frequent food emergencies in our house when there's nothing in the fridge, and Gran doesn't want Jenna or me to have to run down to the chippie to get fish suppers every time.

"And it's going to be hell," Jenna moans predictably, "having to deal with the little horrors on my own for an entire week."

I don't point out that she could have come along if she had wished. It seems silly to start a fight when things are going so well between us. It's a warm June evening and the sea air smells salty and fresh. I feel light with happiness.

"You'll be fine, Jenna," I say, though I can see that it will be hard at home without Gran. She is a very bossy woman, but always a safe, reassuring presence. There are rarely emergencies of any kind when Gran is around.

"And we'll be back before you know it. I'll bring you a stick of Millport rock!" I add brightly.

"Oh thanks. Yum," says Jenna. "You should feed some of that to Gran. It might shut her up for five minutes."

"She's unbelievable isn't she?" I laugh. "When we went to the supermarket, she stood at the till for twenty minutes telling the girl about the problems she's having with her swollen legs. There was a huge queue behind us by the time she'd run out of ways to describe how ghastly they looked. It was hideously embarrassing."

"Lucky you, trapped in a caravan with her for a week," says Jenna. "I couldn't bear it."

I twitter on, trying to keep the conversation flowing. For months, Jenna has communicated with me in grunts and snarls. This seems like progress.

"Do you know that the smell of sea air is caused by a gas called DMS? It's released by bacteria," I say, a bit desperately. "Which is a bit yucky, isn't it?"

"Shut up, Lily," snaps Jenna, and she marches on ahead. So much for progress.

I should still be feeling happy and excited about the approaching holidays, but the ghost is having none of that. On Wednesday morning she turned up in my actual bedroom, while I was in my actual bed.

Being haunted definitely brings a person down.

She has a real body now, though it's creepily faint and, well, ghost-like, and I can't decide whether it's more or less spooky now that she isn't just a disembodied voice. There is certainly no getting away from her. I'm just hoping that she can't travel over water.

On Wednesday, when the ghost appeared in my bedroom, it was about six o'clock in the morning. I was snuggled under my duvet, woken far too early by Bronx's loud and revolting snoring, and worrying about missing out on the school service on the last day of term.

We've been learning a rubbish song about new beginnings that Mrs McKenzie claims is very touching. She says it'll have the parents in floods of tears. If Gran was at the service I know she'd be in tears of laughter. She'd say it was a soppy dirge. Gran has no time for soppiness.

As well as learning the song, everybody in the class has to prepare a few lines about what primary school has meant to them and their plans for the future. Well, everybody in the class except me. Mrs McKenzie said it was a bit pointless if I wasn't going to be at the service. She made me feel really bad about it on Monday, and got me sharpening pencils and tidying the library corner while everyone else got to dream about the future.

It made me wish that my gran had asked me how I felt about leaving primary school before she organised this holiday.

Anyway, when I was lying in bed that morning thinking about school, I got that horrible feeling again that I was being watched.

I turned over in bed and pretended to be asleep, a bit

unsure if ghosts can be fooled by stuff like that. With the covers half over my head, I opened my eyes, but couldn't see anything unusual. I couldn't actually see very much at all, so I pulled my duvet to the side and was about to sit up in bed when there she was by the window, grey and fuzzy in the early morning light.

She was so blurry and faint that I didn't really feel afraid, until she spoke, very softly, in that quiet, strangely familiar voice. It's what she said to me that was scary: "If you can hear me, please listen. Don't go away. Don't go to Millport. Please stay safe, Lily."

"Who are you?" I asked, springing out of bed as if I'd just touched an electric fence. "Why don't you leave me alone?"

But I was too late. She vanished. One minute she was there, and the next she wasn't. I wish she'd stop doing that. I'm sure it's just for effect. She's more melodramatic than Jenna in a strop.

So at school I am on high alert, waiting for her to reappear. I am ready, determined to tackle her head on. What am I afraid of, after all? She's a girl, about the same age as me. Not a terrifying, slathering zombie. My ghost isn't that scary; she isn't threatening to eat my brains or rip out my heart. She might not even be an actual ghost.

But she is very persistent.

Unlike Wednesday morning, this morning was a spook-free zone, but I'm keeping my guard up, determined not to be freaked out by an unexpected visit. All this vigilance is making me a bit jumpy, and when David prods me in the back with a paintbrush, I shriek and leap in the air.

David's so worked up about his latest art installation (a vast model boat) that he doesn't even notice he has nearly given me heart failure. He hands me the paintbrush, which is dripping with brown paint.

"Lily McLean, do I have to paint this entire Viking longship by myself? Or are you going to give me a hand? It was your daft idea to make it life size, after all."

"It isn't life size, you eejit. It wouldn't fit in the classroom if it was. It's still impressive, though."

David surveys his handiwork and nods happily.

"I've painted the figurehead to look like Big Cheryl," he says cheerfully. "It's terrifying, isn't it? Now, take this brush and help me paint the hull. It needs to be finished in time for the school dance, otherwise the Viking-themed decorations are going to look a bit pathetic. We've only got the shields and that big axe Doug made. And the axe might not be allowed."

"Sorry, Dave. I can't just now. Thursday afternoon is library duty. I promise I'll help you finish the ship tomorrow."

I give him back the paintbrush and scurry out, relieved to have an excuse. I head straight for the school library. On

Thursday afternoons it's my duty to prevent the younger pupils from tearing all the books to shreds or causing an avalanche as they drag them off the shelves.

Suddenly, I notice my ghost, drifting bubble-like outside a classroom, lying in wait. As soon as I see her flitting down the corridor towards me, I pounce.

"Who are you? What do you want?" I demand in my loudest, angriest voice, which only trembles a little.

"Lily! Is everything all right?"

I spin round and see Mrs McKenzie a few steps behind me, laden with textbooks and jotters. She is looking aghast, as if I had suddenly announced to the class that I hated school and thought teachers were dumb.

I struggle to think of a good excuse for standing in the corridor, shouting at the walls, but this time I am stumped, and the truth isn't an option. I decide to pretend nothing unusual has happened.

"Hi Mrs McKenzie, I was just heading to the library. Do you want a hand carrying those books?" I ask brightly.

"That would be very helpful, thank you Lily. I'm just going to the staffroom to get a coffee to sustain me while I mark the spelling tests."

I'm sure I hear her add, under her breath, that a stiff gin might be more effective.

Mrs McKenzie hands me a pile of jotters and we walk towards the staffroom together.

"You know, Lily, I've been meaning to talk with you. I am so sorry that you will be missing the end-of-year service. I think it's such an important life event, even more than the Leavers' Dance. It's your chance to say goodbye to primary school properly, rather than just walking out the door at three o'clock as usual and then never coming back. I wish your family could have organised your gran's holiday for another time, I really do."

She stops at the door of the staffroom.

"And we will all really miss you, Lily, in our last week. You have been such an asset to the school, and so patient and kind with the younger pupils."

I blush, thinking of my grumpiness with Bronx and Hudson recently. They can be such little twerps when they don't want to get out of their beds.

"You have admirable strength and resilience you know," continues Mrs McKenzie. "I am absolutely sure you will do very well at secondary and in your future career, whatever you decide to do."

Mrs McKenzie takes the jotters from me and leaves me standing there, bursting with silent pride. She's the second person to tell me this week that I'm a strong person, strong and resilient. Maybe I really can be anything, do anything.

All the same, I'm relieved to see that the ghost has vanished from the corridor. I'm not that flippin' strong.

Chapter 8

Reasons I'm glad to be going on holiday:

- ⭐ I won't have to wear that ghastly pink dress to the Leavers' Dance.
- ⭐ I'll get a week off from Bronx's snoring.
- ⭐ I might be able to leave the ghost behind in Largs.

So today, finally, is my last day of primary school. Mrs McKenzie is right: it isn't going to feel that special when I'm the only one leaving. But I feel quite excited all the same. And tomorrow, I will be on the ferry to Millport.

Rowan and David are already in the playground when I arrive, dragging a reluctant Bronx, at five to nine. While Hudson seems oblivious to everything but computer games, Bronx is in a mutinous rage because I get to finish school early while they have another week to go.

"It's not fair, Lily! You always get to do fun stuff with Gran. Nobody takes me on holiday. Why can't I go too?"

"When you're a bigger boy, I'm sure Gran will take you and Hudson instead of me," I say, hoping I don't sound too doubtful.

Bronx shakes his head. He knows very well that Gran will do no such thing.

I tell him to go and play with his little friends and he stomps off, muttering about the injustice of it all, into the milling throng of tiny P1 kids. I feel really envious of the boys, having all these years of primary school ahead of them.

But I also feel quite sad for them too, that they won't be going anywhere on holiday this summer, or any other, probably, unless Mum buys a winning lottery ticket.

"OMG! I can't believe it! It's going to be so much fun!"

Rowan is leaping about over by the bicycle racks, shrieking excitedly with Georgia, Danielle and Jade. They sound like a flock of squawking macaws. It doesn't take long for me to overhear the reason for all the hysterics. Rowan's mum has given in about the limo, apparently. Some parents have no backbone.

David is standing alone by the fence, running his hands through his unruly hair and looking thoroughly fed up.

"Oh there you are at last," he says gloomily, when I walk over to him. He points over at Rowan and the other girls, who are still screeching at ear-harming decibel levels.

"This is a vision of things to come at high school, you know. Rowan will be sucked into the popular crowd. She'll shake us off like fleas."

"That's not fair, David!" I argue, feeling stung both on Rowan's behalf and on my own. "We've been friends forever. Nothing's going to change. You'll see."

David looks unconvinced.

"Look at her, Lil. She fits right in. We don't. We will be lumped in with the geeks and the nerds and the untouchables, or whatever they call the unpopular kids, while Rowan swans off with the populars. It's inevitable."

I look over at the girls again. Rowan's netball friends are giggling frantically as they gather in a celebratory group hug. Danielle is taking mass pouting selfies on her mobile. Mrs McKenzie will have a fit if she sees that someone has brought a phone to school.

Perhaps David is right and Rowan will leave us behind when we all go off to high school. I hope desperately that she won't. What would I do without my best friend in the world?

Rowan notices us and comes running over, her face glowing with joy.

"I hear you're going to the ball in your golden coach after all, Cinderella," I say. "I take it you didn't have to kill your mum first. I'm sure she mentioned something about you only getting in a hired limo 'over her cold, dead body.'"

"No, it wasn't necessary to go quite that far. I cried, a lot, and that did the trick," replies Rowan, cheerfully. "My dad folded first. He always does. I'm so happy. It would have been so embarrassing to walk to the dance on my own."

"Yes, it will be utterly humiliating, but I guess I'll survive," says David mock-seriously.

Rowan blushes.

"Oh, you're a boy, Dave, it's different. But all the girls are going in limos. I would have felt a complete freak."

I get that horrible feeling again of becoming disconnected from Rowan. It's as if the radio signal between us is getting weaker. She sometimes says things that she must know are shallow, things we would have laughed about before, if some other girl had said them. But now she says those shallow things and seems quite serious. In those moments we're on completely different wavelengths. And if I can't communicate with Rowan, who do I have left?

"It will be hard for me, all the same, having to walk all that way on my lonesome ownsome," sighs David, clutching his chest for dramatic effect. "If only I could share a limo to the dance with Big Cheryl and her pals. If my mum would just let me get an orange spray tan like Cheryl's, maybe it could still happen."

Rowan and I dissolve in giggles.

"You will have to wear a dress like hers, to really fit in, David," I laugh. "I believe there are many layers of white netting involved and a zillion sequins. And do you even *own* a tiara?"

"Well as a matter of fact I have several," says David, and we all burst out laughing, though for all Rowan and I know, he could be telling the truth.

All of a sudden Rowan stops laughing and grabs our hands. "Oh, I know I'm being a bit ridiculous," she says. "Just ignore me, both of you. I know the whole limo thing is stupid."

So she still has one foot in the real world; we haven't lost her completely. But she doesn't offer to walk up to the dance with David.

Everything and everybody is changing, while I'm desperately wishing my school life could stay the same. I don't want to go to secondary school, with its maze-like corridors, stairs leading in all directions and hundreds of teenagers I don't know and who won't want to know me.

The school bell rings and I line up for the final time. Mrs McKenzie comes out to take in the lines, looking grumpier than she usually does on a Friday.

"Is this a line of P7 pupils, or a troupe of baboons?" she asks grouchily. "In a week you will all be leaving this school. Is this the impression you want to create in secondary?"

I will even miss Mrs McKenzie's sarky comments. I feel sentimental tears gathering and hastily brush them away. It's completely unlike me to cry without a good reason, like my hand being trapped in a door, or being haunted on Largs' seafront. And anyway, if I cry I will draw unwanted attention to myself and Mrs McKenzie is clearly in no mood for nonsense this morning.

We pile into the classroom, but it takes a while to get settled into our seats as there is a fight between Doug the Thug and Big Cheryl. She hits him with her bag as she crashes clumsily towards her seat and he takes offence, swears loudly and shoves her.

"You boggin' pig. You done that on purpose! I'm gonna have ya!" roars Cheryl, lunging at Doug, fists flailing.

I would have been scared to intervene but Mrs McKenzie is afraid of nothing and nobody. She charges into the fray and sorts it out. They are both on final warnings, again.

I suspect Mrs McKenzie will not be sad to see the back of Doug the Thug and Big Cheryl.

Rowan slides into a seat beside me and grins.

"Are you all set for tomorrow?" she whispers, as we pull our maths homework from our bags and hand it to Mrs McKenzie, whose face is now grim.

"You know me. I am uber-organised," I reply. "And I can't wait to see you and David on Friday."

Rowan's face clouds over.

"I'm not sure if we're going to make it," she whispers. "My mum says she doesn't want to waste money on the ferry unless it's a really sunny day. I asked if David and I could go over on our own, but she said 'No way'. And what are the chances of a sunny day? Realistically, pretty low."

I sink down in my seat, feeling totally dejected. I had been looking forward to them coming, to showing them both around the island, even though I know they both probably know it as well as I do.

"Oh well," I mutter. "I'll cross my fingers for sunshine on Friday."

"Lily McLean and Rowan Forrest! I've already asked everyone to come and sit at the Smartboard. I did not intend for you two to have an exemption. Will you girls stop rudely whispering and get yourselves over here now! Or do you already know everything there is to know about prepositions? Perhaps you could come over and enlighten the rest of the class?"

Mrs McKenzie is in full-on sarcastic mode today. The clock hands seem to move extra slowly and by lunchtime I am thoroughly fed up. My last day is not proving to be as enjoyable as I had hoped.

And then it gets worse.

As normal, I go to stand in the queue for my free school meals (I may have mentioned our cash flow issues). Once I've loaded up my tray with pizza, potato wedges and pink milk, I go over to join Rowan and David at the table with their packed lunches. Usually I enjoy my school dinner, but today the pepperoni pizza looks rock hard and the wedges are soggy. Only my pink milk looks appealing, and that's saying something.

"At least the school dinners should be better at high school," I say hopefully, jabbing a straw into my milk carton. "We could take this pizza down to the beach and play frisbee with it."

"We had better go there by limo then," jokes David. "It's the only way to travel apparently."

I giggle, but Rowan's face flushes scarlet.

"Stop going on about it, you two!" she yells, standing up so quickly that her chair falls over.

She stalks off to another table and sits down next to Danielle, who looks surprised but delighted.

For the rest of the afternoon, I worry about falling out with Rowan and Mrs McKenzie tells me off twice for daydreaming. Rowan isn't speaking to David or me, and I feel terrible. When the school bell rings, she leaves hurriedly with Jade, Danielle and Georgia. I expect they're going over to Jade's house to gasp at the overwhelming gorgeousness of Jade's new dress.

I didn't mean that to sound quite so bitter. I guess I'm a little bit jealous.

David and I are left standing at our desks, gathering up our blazers and bags.

"Are you going straight home?" he asks. "Do you want to come into town first so I can see if there's any new Star Wars stuff in?"

"Um, 'fraid not, Dave. I've got to collect my brothers," I say, trying to look genuinely sorry. David will be in the shop until closing time, poring over any interesting finds.

"And I've got something to do here first. I'll see you on Friday, with any luck."

David leaves and I linger in the classroom for a moment, adjusting my bag strap.

"Is everything ok, Lily?" Mrs McKenzie asks, and then her hand flies to her mouth. "Oh, Lily, you should have reminded me this is your last day! I feel awful!"

I shuffle over to her desk, feeling really self-conscious, and pull a card and small box of chocolate mints from my bag, bought with the change from Gran's tenner.

"These are for you," I say awkwardly, stating the obvious

as usual, handing them to her. "You've been a really great teacher. I'll miss you a lot."

"Thank you so much, Lily. That's very kind of you, dear. I have something for you too. I'm so glad I remembered before you left for good!"

Mrs McKenzie goes into her desk drawer and pulls out a small parcel carefully wrapped in pale-blue tissue paper. She places it in my hand. Then she gives me a quick, awkward hug.

"Goodbye, Lily. Enjoy your holiday and good luck in secondary school. Come back and see us all some time."

The boys are kicking gravel at each other by the school gates, waiting impatiently for me to come out. Hudson has grass stains on his knees and a sore-looking graze on his arm. Bronx's polo shirt is smeared in blue paint, tomato from his lunchtime pizza and dribbles of pink milk. Gran will be livid. In his sticky hands, Bronx is holding a junk model of a vehicle – a digger apparently – which is so large and unwieldy that I have to stuff Mrs McKenzie's parcel in my blazer pocket and help him to carry it.

"Can we stop at the park, for a minute, Lily? Please, please, please. Harry is going with his mum and we want to see who can go fastest on the new zip wire. Can we? Can we?" he begs, pulling at me with a still rather sticky hand.

Hudson shrugs and I sigh and agree. To be honest, none of us is in a huge hurry to get to Gran's house. She is bound to be preparing a large 'do and don't' list for me to ensure I don't embarrass her in front of her Millport cronies. *Do answer politely when they ask how you're doing at school. Don't roll your eyes when they say how much you've grown...*

When we arrive at the park, it's already busy with small kids eager to try out the new zip wire. Hudson throws his bag at my feet and rushes to the climbing bars to swing arm over arm like a gibbon, while Bronx shakes off my hand and rushes in the opposite direction, waving frantically at his wee pal Harry. Harry's mum is standing by the swings, chatting to some other mothers. They are all smartly dressed, with shiny well-cut hair and carefully applied makeup. Our mum is nothing like them, with her weird smocks and legging combos, her pointy suede boots and her long, wild red hair. I wonder if the boys mind.

I find an unoccupied bench, place our school bags and the junk model digger carefully on it and flop down. It's a dull, overcast day, threatening rain. We'll need to leave in ten minutes in case we get caught in a downpour. I figure that Bronx will freak out if his precious cardboard digger is ruined by the rain.

"I was much faster than you, Harry!" I hear Bronx shriek.

"You were not, you big liar!"

I think this game is not going to end well.

It's a bit chilly sitting on the bench, and the wood is damp against my bare legs. I'm feeling miserable about the fact that primary school is over, for me at least, and really afraid that I might not see my best friend again until we start secondary in August. And maybe she won't speak to me ever again. Perhaps David is right and this is the end of our friendship with Rowan. I remind myself sternly that David has a tendency to be dramatic and that I'm doing the exact same thing.

Then I remember Mrs McKenzie's parcel and slip it quickly from my blazer pocket. I tear at the fragile tissue paper, find a tiny white cardboard box and prise it carefully apart. Inside, there's a little silver-coloured charm in the shape of a flower. I turn it in my hands and see that it's a water lily. Once I've attached it to my school bag I sit back on the bench and admire it, feeling really touched by Mrs McKenzie's thoughtfulness.

Then I realise there is somebody sitting next to me on the bench.

Oh, surely not. Could this day get any worse?

My ghost is perched beside Bronx's model digger, her face turned towards me. I can see her colourless features as if through frosted glass. She has wide eyes, a small, heart-shaped face and long, wavy hair. Today she's wearing what looks like a school uniform. That's weird. Do ghosts change their clothes? Do ghosts go to school?!

She is clutching something tightly in her hands, but I can't tell what it is.

I still can't place who she reminds me of. I can see that she looks very unhappy though.

"What's up with you?" I ask her quietly, trying to speak like a ventriloquist so the parents nearby don't think I'm talking to myself. I am presuming nobody else can see her and that she is picking exclusively on me, since nobody is screaming and pointing out that there's a ghost sitting on one of the park benches.

"Lily, can you really hear me? Can you really see me? Is this real?"

Oh great. I'm being haunted by a ghost who doesn't even know she's doing it.

"Well of course I can hear you. I'm not deaf and you keep hissing in my ear! And I can sort of see you, but you're a bit fuzzy, to be honest." I'm really going for it now. "And why are you always so flamin' worried looking?" I snap at her when she doesn't reply, forgetting for a moment that I'm not alone in the park. "Why don't you want me to go to Millport? I go every year with my gran, and you haven't ever interfered before. It's not really your business, is it, what I do? I don't even know you. Leave me alone."

"It *is* my business, *listen* to me," she replies sadly. "Don't go to Millport. Stay away from the water, Lily."

She looks at me beseechingly and as I stare back into her wide dark eyes, trying to remember where I have heard her voice before, she fades and disappears. I am left on my own, sitting in the drizzle on a park bench.

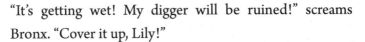

"It's getting wet! My digger will be ruined!" screams Bronx. "Cover it up, Lily!"

He runs over to rescue it from the rain, which is now falling hard.

"Ha! Your model's all mushy," taunts Hudson as he skids up to us.

Ignoring both of them, I scoop the digger and our school bags into my arms and we start to race out of the park and up the road towards Gran's house. Our hair is getting soaked and our clothes sodden. We will all be a crumpled, soggy mess by the time we get there, digger included.

"Harry says he was fastest, but it was definitely me," Bronx shouts as he runs. "Did you see me, Lil? Sure I was faster than Harry?"

"Yes, you were fast as an asteroid heading straight for Earth!" I call back, and Bronx grins happily.

I glance down at my school bag with its water lily charm. "Stay away from the water, Lily." Were the ghost's words some kind of code? Or is she a figment of my imagination? Gran is always telling me that I have an overactive imagination. But if I am inventing a ghost, and managing to scare myself with it, there's definitely something wrong with me.

I think that, on balance, I would rather she was real.

Chapter 9

Today's major events:

* ⭐ Millport! Yay!
* ⭐ Gran is a nightmare. An embarrassing nightmare.
* ⭐ I meet a girl on the ferry, and she's real, for a change.

My holdall doesn't do anything of the kind. There are loads of other things I want to pack and there's no more room in the stupid thing. And anyway, I'm out of time. Gran will be here any minute to whisk me away to a tropical paradise. (I wish.)

I stand at the window, bulging holdall at my feet, and wait. The holdall looks good: black and glossy, with my water lily charm attached to the zip. I'm wearing a Peanuts t-shirt, my new skinny jeans and my bright orange shoes.

"You look great, Lily," says Mum. "Really cool."

I wish my mum would not try and use words like 'cool'. It's just embarrassing.

Mum is on the couch, holding Summer firmly on her lap while she struggles to dress her. Summer has learned some new words and is using them all at once.

"No, no, no, no!" she yells furiously. "No socks. No shoes. Feet!"

Mum sighs deeply.

"Come on, Summer, co-operate with me. You can't walk about in your bare feet."

"No socks! Bad socks! Bad Mum!"

"It was easier when she couldn't speak," grumbles Mum, as Summer pulls the tiny socks off her feet and stuffs them down the front of Mum's jumper.

"No socks," she burbles happily. "Socks gone 'way. Bye-bye socks."

Bronx and Hudson come charging in, throw themselves on the couch and almost catapult Summer into the air.

"For goodness' sake, be careful," shouts Mum, but Summer just laughs and bounces up and down on Mum's knee. She seems happier since she started to talk. Life is probably a lot less frustrating when you can explain what you want. I hope she isn't too lonely this week without me. I'll miss her.

"Lily, will you bring me a present from Mapes?" wheedles Bronx, tugging at my hand. Mapes is the toy shop in Millport – the boys are obsessed with it. "I'd like a lightsabre, or a sword, or a gun that shoots foam discs. Or one with real bullets would be better."

"I'm sure you would, Bronx, but I don't have enough spending money for a big present. I'll get you some sweeties or maybe a lucky bag from Mapes, as long as you've been a good boy for Jenna and Mum."

"Me, too?" pleads Hudson. "Can I have an ice cream with a flake and raspberry sauce?"

"I think that might melt by the time I get it home on the ferry," I laugh. The boys are quite funny when they're not rampaging around, causing havoc.

I worry suddenly that a week is quite a long time for them to manage without me.

"Right lads," I say sternly. "What are the Three Unbreakable Rules?"

Bronx waves his arm in the air, as though he's in the classroom, but Hudson shouts out excitedly.

"We must change our pants and socks every day cos else we'll get smelly!"

"Yup. And Bronx?"

"We need to brush our teeth twice a day cos if we don't they will get yellow and disgusterous."

"And the Third Unbreakable Rule?"

"I know, I know!" screeches Hudson. "We must never cross roads on our own, even if there's a zillion pound note on the other side."

"Because a zillion pounds is no use if we are squished flat, like that hedgehog you showed us," finishes Bronx.

I might even miss my wee brothers this week. They are quite cute looking, with their floppy fair hair, big grey eyes and freckled noses.

"Can I use your bed as a den while you're away, Lil?" asks Bronx.

"No, I'm having it!" yells Hudson and he flings himself on Bronx and starts to pummel him with his fists. "I need it for Swampfire."

I have no idea what he's talking about, but it doesn't sound good. My brothers are aliens. Not cute at all.

Bronx bawls and aims a flying kick at Hudson, who crumples, wailing and clutching his stomach.

I take it all back. I won't miss them one bit. Not one tiny subatomic particle.

"If either of you lay one finger on my bed, or on any of my stuff, the television remote will magically dissolve and you will never be able to find it again," I warn them and then quickly shoo them to the side as the doorbell rings. Gran's here!

I rush to the door and fling it open. She is standing on the step, wearing her beige raincoat and carrying her enormous patent-leather handbag. Her battered brown case is propped at her feet, and she already looks puffed out from the effort of carrying it.

"Right, Lily. Are you ready to go?" she asks brusquely. "I'm not coming in. So get a move on."

I rush back into the living room and grab my holdall and anorak. Mum puts Summer down and gives me a big hug.

"I hope you have a lovely time, pet," she says, kissing my forehead. "Take care of yourself. Be good for your gran."

"I will, Mum, promise," I say brightly, and bounce backwards towards the door, waving frantically.

Bronx and Hudson are now sitting together on the couch, smiling sweetly and waving, a suspicious picture of grey-eyed innocence. As soon as the door closes behind me, I know they will be dragging the covers off my bed to make their den. I click an imaginary remote to remind them of my threat.

Jenna is standing at the foot of the stairs. She reaches out, grabs my hand and shoves a five-pound note into it.

"Have a good time, Lil. Better you than me," she whispers, waving at Gran, who is still standing in the doorway, her face grumpy with impatience.

Jenna runs back up the stairs and I stand dumbly watching her, too astonished to shout thanks.

The walk down to the pier takes a long time, as I am lugging both my heavy holdall and Gran's case, which I can barely lift. We have to keep stopping so I can have a wee rest. My arms feel as though they are being wrenched from their sockets.

"Come on Lily. Get a move on, girl," urges Gran as she strides ahead, her big bottom wobbling as she walks. "We haven't got all day."

When we finally arrive at the pier, the ferry is just coming in. Gran goes to buy our tickets and I watch the big bow door clank like a monster's jaw onto the stone ramp and spit the cars out one by one.

There are a lot of foot passengers and cyclists waiting to hand over their tickets and Gran is determined to be at the head of the queue.

"Hurry up, Lily. Follow me!" she shouts. "I need to get a seat on the ferry, or my old legs will swell up like balloons."

She shoves her way to the front and I cringe with embarrassment. Then she drops her tickets in the man's outstretched hand, and stomps down the ramp. I scuttle after her, dragging both bags. Once on board, Gran finds a seat downstairs and I plonk the bags down beside her.

"Oh, I'm shattered," she gasps, fanning her face with one plump hand. "That walk was exhausting. The ruddy case weighs a ton."

I shake my head in amazement and rub my sore arms.

"I'm going to sit up top, Gran. Is that ok?" I ask, and she

nods in agreement, clearly keen to engage the elderly lady in the seat across from her in conversation. The poor old woman is trapped, wedged in by Gran's heap of bags and jackets. I hope for her sake she has a hearing aid she can switch off.

"You wouldn't believe the trouble I have with my digestion," confides my gran, in a stage whisper. "I'm a martyr to migraine, too. And as for my blood pressure. The doctor says he's never seen such…"

I shake my head again in disbelief at Gran's idea of a conversation opener. The old woman tries to edge closer to the ferry window.

It's only when I'm standing at the railings, the sea breeze whipping my hair and salt spray splashing the sides of the ferry, that I remember the ghost's warning to stay away from water.

Oh dear. I'm not exactly taking her advice. But what harm can I possibly come to?

I look nervously over the rail, down at the frothy, churning firth. I could lose my balance and topple in. Somebody could deliberately push me and I'd plunge down into the dark, foaming water and perhaps be sucked under the hull of the ferry. These are scary thoughts.

I turn my head towards the green hills of Cumbrae. It's going to be ok. We're nearly there already. The slipway is ahead and I can see the familiar blue bus waiting at the stop.

It will be weird being in Millport without Jenna, but I am determined to enjoy myself. There are no alternative holidays on offer, so I need to make the absolute best of this one. And I can get away with not going in the sea. Swimming in it isn't that enjoyable anyway, as it's so piercingly cold. I cross my fingers and hope that I have left the ghost behind in Largs.

"Wishing yourself luck, are you?" says a voice at my ear. I jump in the air, startled. There's a girl standing next to me. Not a ghostly girl, a real live one, with short jet-black hair and eyes as soft and brown as chocolate buttons.

"Wow, that's an overactive startle response," says the girl, frowning mock-seriously. "I diagnose some kind of terrible trauma requiring a long period of rest and recuperation. How long are you staying for? I would recommend a month for a full cure."

"Oh, just a week," I reply, a bit warily. "I come every year with my gran. What about you?"

"I live here," says the girl. "All year round. I'm a prisoner on this island. The guards let me out on occasional accompanied visits to the mainland, if I've been well behaved and kept my cell clean."

I giggle. She is funny, this girl, and I'm always impressed by people who can make me laugh. I also love her bright, eccentric clothes. She wears a loose apple-green cotton top and fuschia-pink velvet shorts with rainbow-striped socks and lace-up walking boots.

"My name's Lily," I tell her. "I'm from Largs. My mum believes I need to see the world so she has sent me on this eight-minute voyage to a faraway land. I'm only to come back if I succeed in making my fortune."

"There aren't many ways of getting rich in Millport," grins the girl. "You might be here for a while, after all. Where are you staying?"

"My gran has booked a caravan, out towards Fintry Bay," I reply, suddenly wondering how Gran and I are going to make it there with our luggage.

"Maybe I'll see you around. The guards allow me a short period of daily exercise," she says, grinning widely at me. "I live on Stuart Street, next to the Wedge. Britain's skinniest house! I'm Aisha, by the way."

She turns away and clumps down the metal ferry steps, two at a time. The doors are being lowered. They clang onto the slipway, and I follow Aisha down the steps, back to Gran.

As I lug the cases up the slipway and on to the bus, followed by a puffing, red-in-the-face Gran, I hear a shout and turn to see Aisha waving from the open back window of a silver Audi.

"Good luck with seeking your fortune!" she yells. "Let's meet up tomorrow. About eleven o'clock, by the pier!"

I wave back, and can feel myself grinning widely. Maybe I won't be lonely on this holiday after all.

Gran shoos a boy off his seat so she can sit down near the front of the bus.

"Move your lazy carcass," she demands. "You shouldn't be sitting down when there's a poor frail old lady having to stand."

The boy's mother glares and mutters, but doesn't argue with my gran. Few people are brave enough to do that. The bus rumbles along the narrow, winding road and I cling to a metal post to prevent myself being tossed to the floor. The driver seems determined to break our necks and as the bus swings round every bend, I imagine us swerving off the road onto the rocky shore. Gran clutches the bar in front of her seat and criticises the driver's skills loudly enough for everyone, including him, to hear.

"Lily, don't let go of that bar. The man's a maniac!" she yells, and I blush with mortification.

I gaze out at the rocky foreshore, hoping for a glimpse of a grey seal, but the only wildlife I can see are the hordes of gulls and a small group of pretty sandpipers, their heads bobbing as they search for insects on the rocks. As the bus drives past an enormous lump of volcanic rock shaped like a squatting lion, I squirm with excitement in my seat. We're nearly there!

"Gran, look, there's the Lion Rock!" I can't resist saying, even though she can hardly miss seeing it.

An elderly man looks up at me from his seat and smiles.

"It was meant to be a bridge to the mainland, but when the elves realised they couldn't finish it, they kicked big holes in it," he told me, his eyes twinkling. "That's why there are no elves on this side of the island. But there are plenty left in Fintry Bay."

"Bill McInnes, don't you be telling my granddaughter daft fairy tales," retorts my gran. And then, delighted to find someone she knows, she starts relaying all of her ailments to him.

"I've had a terrible year, Bill," she begins, with grim satisfaction. "My arthritis has been playing up something terrible. You would not like to see how swollen my joints are on a bad day…"

I bet the poor man wishes he hadn't opened his mouth to speak to me.

Finally, the bus arrives in Millport town and I stare out of the grimy window at familiar landmarks: Crocodile Rock, the garishly painted boulder which only vaguely resembles a reptile; the ancient crazy golf course; the smartly renovated Garrison library and museum; Mapes' bike hire and toy shop; the Ritz café and, at last, the old pier, so crumbly that it is due to be demolished.

"Gran, we need to get off the bus," I say urgently, because she is so busy discussing her aches and pains with old Bill that the bus could turn and head back to the jetty before she'd notice.

"Oh, you're right enough, Lil," agrees Gran amiably. She is being unusually pleasant to me and I wonder if she is trying to impress Bill. Maybe she fancies him. What a gruesome thought.

We stagger off the bus when it stops at the pier and begin the difficult trek to the caravan site, me lugging both bags and Gran wheezing along behind me, complaining with every step. Then, to my huge relief, a car slows down beside us and the driver shouts for us to get in.

It's one of the local ladies Gran has got to know over the years and the woman kindly gives us a lift out to the site. I can't thank her enough, as I think I would have ended up carrying Gran as well as the bags if we'd had to walk.

"How's your Bert doing, Gladys?" asks Gran, when she has squeezed herself into the front seat of the tiny Fiat. I'm crushed in the backseat with all the bags and Flora, an enormously fat, foul-breathed spaniel, who keeps trying to use me as a comfy cushion.

"Oh, it's been terrible, Morag. He has had three minor attacks since Christmas. He's not a well man. He sits there in his armchair looking out the window all day long. And I say to him, Bert, you'll have a proper heart attack if you don't get out that chair and take a bit of exercise now and then."

I can imagine the contentment stealing across Gran's face. Nothing seems to make her happier than talking about illness.

"Oh, that's terrible, Gladys. I have a dicky heart myself. I thought that walk with those heavy cases might be the death of me."

It might have been, if you'd actually been carrying them, I think grumpily, glancing down at the red marks on my hands.

"It's lovely to see your wee granddaughter again. Milly, is it? She's grown like a weed since last summer! How are you getting on at school, dear?"

"Lily's top of her class in English," says Gran, answering for me with a big fat fib. "She starts high school in August."

"She'll be at university soon, I expect. Won't you, Milly?"

I sigh with relief when I realise we've arrived at the caravan site. I push Flora off my knee, drag the bags out of the back seat, thank Gladys and help Gran to heave herself out of the car.

We're here!

I have a feeling Gran won't want to travel far from the caravan this week and I hope I'm not going to be stuck in the campsite the whole time, keeping her company.

We've stayed at this site before and Gran knows the owners. As she heads in to collect the keys she stops for a chat and I sigh and sit on the case, waiting for her to finish yapping. A warm breeze is blowing through the long grass and I can hear bees buzzing. It's very quiet and peaceful, but I worry that it might be really, really boring out here.

It feels like a lifetime before we finally reach our big green caravan. Propped outside is a smart shiny blue bike.

"That's for you to use while we're here," says Gran. "I organised it through the site owners so that you can get out and about. I want you to have a great holiday. You're a good girl, Lily."

I wrap my arms round my gran's plump middle and give her an enormous squeeze.

"Thanks so much, Gran! It's fantastic. I thought I would just be hiring a bike by the hour now and then. I never thought I would have one all to myself for the whole week!"

We explore the large, comfortable caravan, which takes all of five minutes.

"Can I have this room, Gran?" I ask, pointing to the middle-sized bedroom.

It has bunk beds with green floral duvets and sunshine-yellow curtains. I throw my fake Gucci holdall on the bottom bunk and then undo my water lily charm and attach it to one of the belt loops on my jeans.

I look around, feeling pretty pleased with myself. It is going to be bliss having a room of my own for a week and a bike to cycle into Millport when the caravan site is too quiet.

Gran calls me to come outside and admire the view. It's

glorious. Sunlight is sparkling on the firth. High in the sky a buzzard is circling. Gran squeezes her ample bottom into a folding chair and closes her eyes.

"I'm just going to have a wee nap, Lily. That was a tiring journey."

I think how much worse it could have been if that kind woman hadn't given us a lift.

"Would you like me to head back into town and get us some supplies?" I ask, desperate to be out exploring on my bike.

Gran agrees, hands me some money out of her huge handbag, and goes back to snoozing happily in the sunshine, head curled like a giant dormouse.

I cycle out into open countryside, sea on one side of me and grassy hills on the other. White-sailed yachts skim through the water, trails of spray left in their wake. It's so quiet that all I can hear is the mewing call of the buzzard and the slap of waves breaking against the rocks.

This is going to be so much fun, especially if the weather stays sunny. But I know that if I wish for a week of sunshine I'm tempting fate. This is Scotland, after all.

When I come to a small beachy inlet, I steer the bike on to the grass and jump down to the sand. Shoes pulled off, I dip one foot in the sea and withdraw it immediately. Perhaps not. The water is freezing – absolutely Baltic.

"Lily McLean!" shouts a cross voice behind me. I whirl round, and find myself almost nose to nose with the ghost. She can swim after all. Or maybe she took the ferry and the bus, like a normal person.

"Will you stop creeping up on me!" I yell, recovering from my fright. "You keep telling me something bad is going to happen, and then you scare me half to death! If I have a heart attack, it will totally be your fault."

"I ask you not to go near water, but you don't listen!" she says, sounding angry and desperate. "Why won't you listen? I'm trying to keep you alive!"

"It's only my big toe, for goodness' sake," I retort. "I don't breathe through my toes. The rest of me is still up here in the fresh air. Stop stressing! You're dead already, you might as well chill. It's all over."

"I'm not dead," she says, in a shocked voice. "What are you on about?"

I can see her a little more clearly than last time. Today she is wearing jeans and a t-shirt. How often do ghosts change their clothes? Her eyes are dark and glistening with tears. Suddenly I feel guilty about being so grumpy with her. She seems so slight and vulnerable. And I shouldn't have said that about it being all over for her. She clearly doesn't realise she's a ghost.

"Look, if you will stop haunting me, I promise that I will stay away from the water all week," I say, more gently. "It's a total pain, because this is my summer holiday, and I am on a little island surrounded by the sea on all sides, but if it keeps you happy and out of my hair, I will promise."

She smiles as I say these words. She has a really lovely smile, which lights up her face. It has an actual glow, or perhaps that's just the sun shining through her. She's still almost transparent.

"Thank you, Lily," she whispers. "Thank you so much. You have no idea how much that means to me."

I suddenly feel desperately sorry for her. Poor little thing. Maybe she died in an epidemic of plague or an outbreak of cholera or typhus or something. Kids were always catching stuff like that in the olden days. They didn't wear t-shirts and jeans though.

She slowly fades and leaves me standing, alone and barefoot on the deserted beach. I back away from the gently lapping waves. I have made her a promise, and I intend to keep it. Besides, the sea is absolutely freezing anyway. And if it means she will leave me alone, I can avoid the water this holiday. I slip my shoes back on, get on my bike and head into Millport to buy teabags, butter, bread and a pint of milk for Gran and me. I might even treat myself to a marshmallow ice cream from the Ritz café.

Chapter 10

Reasons why this is a mixed-up kind of day:

* People keep getting my name wrong.
* Aisha seems to enjoy almost getting herself killed.
* She tells me some secrets... but I can't tell her mine.

The next day the weather is overcast and dull, but at least it's not raining – yet. After a big breakfast of toast, square sausages and scrambled eggs, I hang about the caravan with Gran, playing snap and gin rummy, but I can see she is impatient to get rid of me. Yesterday evening, after dinner, Gran went on a wee wander round the campsite and bumped into an elderly woman who is staying in a nearby caravan. The poor old dear has been talked into inviting Gran over for a cup of tea and a chat. By chat, my gran really means that she will talk and the other lady will listen: no interruptions, thank you.

I put on my new shorts, a t-shirt and Jenna's pink cardigan. I clip my water lily charm onto the zip of my backpack.

"I'm going to pop into Millport, Gran. Do you want anything?" I ask.

"Just get me a *Sunday Mail* and some bacon," says Gran. "I'll get the other essentials at the campsite shop tomorrow."

I head off to meet Aisha at the pier.

She isn't there when I arrive and I swing out on my bike to cycle along Stuart Street. The town is Sunday-morning quiet, though I know it will get busier soon when the buses arrive from the ferry. Some of the shops are already open and I go into the newsagents to buy my gran's newspaper. Gladys is standing at the counter, with her big smelly spaniel in tow, chatting to the owner about the weather.

"Oh hello, dear!" she says cheerily. "Agnes, this is Morag's wee granddaughter, Milly. Hasn't she grown since last year?"

Agnes clearly doesn't remember me at all, but agrees that I have indeed grown. I am hardly likely to have shrunk, am I?

I smile, stuff Gran's paper into my backpack and hurry out of the shop.

There's a strong breeze and foamy waves slap against the sea wall. I pass the Wedge – it's so skinny, there's barely room for the front door, though I guess it must widen out towards the back like a slice of pie. I remember Aisha saying that she lives next to the Wedge, but there's no sign of her.

I whizz past the crazy golf and the old fashioned swings, all the way to the Crocodile Rock. I turn there and zoom back along the sea front, loving the feeling of the wind in my hair.

Then I see Aisha, in her butterfly colours, speeding up the pavement on a battered red bicycle towards me.

She does a wheelie as she approaches, and then leaps off the bike. Aisha seems to do everything at a hundred miles an hour.

"Hi, Lily! Good to see you again. I've permission to be absent from the prison for an extended leave, because it's the weekend." She beams at me, catching her breath. "How best to spend this precious time? Do you want to cycle right round the island, go rock-pooling round the Crocodile Rock or head out on my brother's rowing boat?"

I think for a moment. Normally, I'd jump at the chance of going out in a boat. We could have rowed over to Little Cumbrae. It would be really exciting. But...

I'm not a crazy person, but if somebody warns you not

to do something and you get the feeling you might die if you do it, the sensible thing is to listen to that warning. Even if they are a ghost, or a figment of your imagination. My ghost has warned me to stay away from water, and I'm keeping my promise.

"Let's go for a cycle," I say. "I'm really keen to try out this bike."

I think Aisha looks a tiny bit disappointed, but she agrees that a bike ride will be great and we set off.

She cycles faster than anyone I have ever met, possibly faster than proper cyclists like the ones in the Olympics. We are lucky the roads are quiet, because Aisha has clearly not passed her Bikeability training at school. She rides in the middle of the road and swerves out in front of traffic. She's a bit crazy, to be honest. I'm beginning to think that the rowing boat would have been a safer option.

"Hey, did you see that lunatic of a van driver!" she yells from up ahead. "He shook his fist at me!"

"That's because you were lurching over on to his side of the road and he thought you were going to come crashing through his windscreen, Aisha!" I shout. "Be careful or you'll end up on the beach!"

Aisha veers off the grass and bounces back on to the gravel verge, her tyres skidding dangerously.

"Why don't we stop and have an ice cream at Fintry Bay?" I suggest.

"Yeah, good plan," she replies, her wheels wobbling madly when she turns her head to speak to me. "Race you there."

I groan, and try and keep up with her, but she is scarily indifferent to other road users and I can't follow her without risking my life. We are cycling uphill when Aisha suddenly veers out into the centre of the road on a blind bend. A car is coming in the other direction. There's a screech of brakes and a crunching of tyres on gravel as the car swerves into the verge to avoid her. Aisha teeters and tumbles off the bike in a weird slow motion fall. Her bike lies on the gravel, its back wheel spinning.

The driver leaps from his car and runs over, his face white.

"Is she ok? Is she ok?" he asks repeatedly. "She was right in the middle of the bloomin' road!"

I have already abandoned my bike and now I run across the road to where Aisha is lying on her back on the grassy verge. As I approach, she stands up, rubs the grass and gravel off her knees and hops over to where her bike is lying.

"Is it damaged?" she asks anxiously. The car driver looks as if he is about to combust.

"You stupid girl!" he yells. "You could've been killed! Until you learn to ride that thing properly, keep off the bloomin' roads!"

Aisha looks at him calmly.

"There's no need to shout," she says reproachfully, her big chocolate-brown eyes glistening with tears. "I'm sorry I gave you a fright. I had to swerve to avoid hitting a wee rabbit that had run out on the road."

I stare at her, amazed. I thought I could tell a lie fairly well when necessary, but Aisha is exceptionally good at it. But why put yourself in a situation where you have to lie to get yourself out of trouble? Why not just avoid the trouble in the first place?

The driver is completely taken in and backs down immediately. He checks that she is unhurt and the bike undamaged and then goes on his way.

Aisha grins at me as she wipes at her knee with a tissue. The blood is trickling from a graze on to her stripy socks.

"Yikes, that was close. Think we'd better be a bit more careful, don't you? No more racing, Lily!"

I resent the suggestion that she fell off her bike because we were racing. The accident was all her own fault. She must know that. At this point I think she realises I'm annoyed with her.

"Oh cheer up, Lil!" she calls, getting back on her bike and wobbling up the hill. "Last one to the café buys the ice cream!"

I get on my bike and follow, my feet pedalling hard, enjoying the speed as I crest the hill and zip down the other side towards Fintry Bay café.

We sit on the wide grass verge, licking ice lollies (which I had to buy). The café is busy, mainly due to the arrival of a crowd of people wearing fancy dress on a charity cycle ride around the island. They shake their bucket in our direction, but I just smile and shake my head. My holiday funds are very limited.

"I can't afford to give to charity, either," says Aisha glumly. "My family are so poor, we are virtually scavenging in skips."

I can't tell if she is joking or not, so don't reply. Aisha keeps talking. She could give my gran a run for her money, but I don't mind. It means I don't have to try too hard and there are no awkward silences.

"I'm thinking of setting up my own charity. I could build a website, describe myself as a poor, destitute orphan and accept donations by debit card or Paypal. I'll call it 'Action for Aisha', or something."

"I'm not sure that's exactly legal," I say, a bit primly. Aisha ignores me.

"We are so squashed in our flat, too," she continues, self pityingly. "Now that Imran has to have his own bedroom for 'studying', I've got to share with my wee brother, Aziz, and he's a total ned. You'll never guess what he did to me last week!"

"What did he do?" I ask curiously, wondering if her wee brother could possibly be as gruesome as my two.

"He went into my underwear drawer, which is bad enough," says Aisha, and I think of my own underwear drawer, with my lovely new bra tucked at the back. I would have a fit if Bronx and Hudson went in there. Come to think of it, they're probably raking through the drawer right now, taking my bra out and using it as a hammock for their action figures. "But worse than that," she continues. "Aziz took out my top-secret diary and broke the lock. Then he leafed through the whole book until he found a part he could actually read, which was amazing, as he's thick as a brick. And then the wee swine showed it to my mum."

"Oh that's bad," I sympathised. "What a wee toad."

"Yes, he is, but that isn't the worst part. The part he showed Mum was written when I was very angry with her. I wrote: 'Mum's a total cow because she won't tell me when Dad's coming back and I wish she was dead.' I'm not proud of writing that, but everybody says things they don't mean when they're angry."

I shudder in sympathy. Her brother does sound like a fiend. But it seems that writing down stuff like that in a diary, or anywhere else, is a pretty dumb thing to do. If you don't want your secrets broadcast, then the only safe place for them is in your own head. Not that people keep secrets any more. Everyone goes on the Jeremy Kyle show and tells the whole world their problems. Everyone except me, that is. I'm keeping my secret to myself. I don't want the whole world creasing itself laughing at 'The Girl Who Thinks She's Being Haunted!'

Aisha is in full flow now.

"Having to share a room with Aziz is a total breach of my human rights. It's cruel and unusual punishment. I should sue my mum!"

"Hey, you're lucky. I have to share with *two* wee brothers!" I interrupt, suddenly keen to get a word in edgeways. "And my big sister has turned into Godzilla overnight. One day she was perfectly normal and pleasant, the next, a monster."

A monster who gave you a fiver to spend when she has hardly any money of her own, I think guiltily.

We lick our ice lollies and sympathise with each other's bad luck. I tell her that my dad is dead, which usually trumps anyone else's sob story, but Aisha has her own tale to tell.

"My dad has vanished," she says, tears in her big brown eyes. I don't know if she's telling the truth or if this is another fairy story, and I think of Rowan, who I can always trust to tell me the truth.

"Dad went to Pakistan nearly three months ago. He said he was going away on business but I'm worried that he isn't coming back," says Aisha sadly. "And the awful thing is, my mum doesn't seem that bothered. She won't tell me what's going on, or when, or even *if* Dad is coming home. I'm really scared that he's decided he prefers living over there. He and Mum did argue a lot."

She puts her face in her hands, and I put my arm awkwardly round her shoulder and pat her on the back.

"I'm sure he'll turn up soon, Aisha," I say, trying to sound confident. "He probably just needs some space or something, what with your flat being so crowded."

"Space away from me, probably," sobs Aisha.

I keep patting her shoulder, hoping that I am doing and saying the right things. I always want to leave the room when people get upset or angry, but I'm outside in the open air and there's no hall cupboard here for me to go and hide in. We are clearly very different, Aisha and me.

I deal with sadness by closing down and keeping quiet, not by sharing my worries with people, never mind people I hardly know.

But there is something very likeable and approachable about Aisha. She is easy to talk to and I have told her a lot about myself today, much more than I usually would. It's somehow easy to be honest with her. Maybe because I don't really know her very well and probably won't see her again after this week.

Of course, I haven't mentioned the ghost. There's a big difference between telling a new friend some basic stuff about yourself and giving away secrets that make them think you're a crazy person. Anyway, Aisha would probably just say that she's being haunted too, and her ghost is far scarier than my ghost.

"So, Lily. You look as if you're about the same age as me. Are you starting high school in August too?" asks Aisha.

I nod, my smile dissolving. "I'm going to Largs Academy. I'm not really looking forward to it," I admit. "Our class went up on the induction days and I found the school a bit big and daunting. And some of the teachers seem quite strict."

"I didn't make it to the induction days. I was off ill with the stupid chicken pox. Imagine getting chicken pox at my age. It was Aziz's fault, cos he gave it to me. It was so embarrassing. I had hideous scabs everywhere, like a plague victim," says Aisha, standing up and doing a zombie walk across the grass.

"Where is the secondary school on Cumbrae?" I ask curiously.

Aisha laughs. "There isn't one, you dope. There aren't nearly enough kids. I'll have to get the ferry over every day to Largs Academy. We'll be at the same school! Won't that be excellent?"

I don't speak for a moment, trying to digest this new information. And then I smile widely.

Aisha is a bit strange and a bit wild, but she is definitely not boring. Secondary school is suddenly a more exciting prospect.

I hope Rowan and David make it over on Friday so they can meet her and that they'll get on with each other. It's always a bit tense trying to mix old friends and new ones.

Chapter 11

Potentially life-changing events:

- ✦ I decide on my future career.
- ✦ Aisha and I fall out.
- ✦ The caravan is hit by a tsunami. (Well, nearly.)

The next few days whizz by, and I love every minute. Aisha has to go to school, of course, but during the day I am happy to hang around the campsite with Gran or explore the island on my own, a pair of borrowed binoculars slung round my neck and carrying a ridiculous-looking, but very useful, fishing net. I'm seriously considering a future career as a marine biologist. Farland Point has some amazing rock pools full of seaweed, barnacles, limpets and tiny crustaceans. I spend hours training my binoculars on groups of oystercatchers and curlews feeding on the beach. I sketch the birds in my red leather notebook and am pretty pleased with the results. Maybe I'll write and illustrate books about nature when I grow up instead.

This gives me plenty of time to write in my journal. I make lots of useful lists and also write a scary sci-fi story about shape-changing aliens, modelled on Bronx and Hudson of course, though my fictional aliens aren't nearly as weird.

There's a little shelf of old paperbacks in the caravan and I sneak some to read, ones that I'm guessing Mrs McKenzie would say are 'inappropriate'. The rude bits are quite interesting but there's a lot of boring nonsense to wade through before you get to them, so I have to do a lot of skimming and scanning.

At four o'clock every day I meet Aisha in the Ritz café and we sit at the Formica tables and eat ice cream or drink hot chocolate, depending on the weather, which is a bit mixed-up. She is always beautifully dressed in bright, designer-type clothes, and I figure that the whole 'scavenging out of skips' story is another of her inventions. She never brings any friends from school, and always looks delighted to see me. I wonder if perhaps Aisha is a bit lonely. Maybe all her storytelling and exaggeration gets on the other kids' nerves.

But I find her easy company, always full of chat. She

tells me funny stories about the kids in her class or about the locals who walk past the café window and she always manages to make me laugh.

"See, that guy there," she whispers, covering her mouth with her hand, and pointing a bit too obviously at a gangly teenager who is shuffling past the window. "He's madly in love with the girl who works in the kitchens at the hotel. She thinks he's a total loser, and when he asked her out she said no. One night, he went and stood with a guitar outside the window of the hotel kitchen and sang her love songs. Imran says it was so bad, the customers all begged him to shut up, but he kept on and on. Anyway, this dog was trotting past and couldn't stand the noise either, so it bit the guy on the bum. And while the boy was hopping about in agony, a seagull pooped right in his hair. He had to go to the hospital for a tetanus injection. That's why he's walking a bit strangely. And the girl from the kitchens still won't go out with him, even after all that."

I burst out laughing, and then feel a bit mean. "Was that a true story, Aisha?" I ask doubtfully.

"All my stories are true," she insists, looking at me reproachfully with her big brown eyes, but I know by now what she's like.

Every day, after our snack in the café, we head off on a mini-adventure. On Monday afternoon we go clambering across some of the rocks on the seashore. It's low tide, so I feel I'm not breaking any promises.

"I dare you to jump from that rock to this one!" shouts Aisha, while I'm happily peering into a deep little pool, hoping I might see a starfish or an anemone.

I accept the dare, which is a silly move because the rock I land on is treacherously slimy with seaweed.

"Help!" I squeal as my feet slide from under me.

One foot skids straight into a pool of brackish water. The other becomes wedged in a narrow crevice. I get a bit panicky for a moment, imagining that this might be how I die, trapped in the rocks as the tide brings the sea ever closer. But I tug hard, and my foot slides out, minus my shoe, which I have to retrieve with a long piece of driftwood. Aisha laughs as I squelch over to show her my bruised ankle.

There seems to be an element of danger in whatever we do. But despite my wet feet and sore ankle, the climbing is good fun and it's a beautiful sunny day. The sun glints on the blue water as dozens of small boats bob around in the bay.

"Who needs the Mediterranean!" shouts Aisha, balanced precariously between two slippery rocks. "We've got Millport!"

"Yup, it even has palm trees," I agree. "It's practically perfect."

As if to remind us that this is Scotland, not Spain, Tuesday is dreich and drizzly, so after hot chocolates in the Ritz, Aisha and I trawl the gift shops.

"I've to get the boys some kind of weapon, preferably one of mass destruction," I tell Aisha, so we head for the toy shop, hoping they will have something suitably lethal-looking.

We find cheapish, powerful water guns, which will have to do, though I know they would have preferred pellet guns or air pistols. I also pick up a sweet little red-haired rag doll in a polka-dot dress, and decide to buy it for Summer, although it's more expensive than I'd like.

"She'll love this," I say, showing it to Aisha. "It actually looks a bit like her. Wee Summer's got bright red hair and little beady eyes too."

"She sounds just darling," mocks Aisha, and I nearly choke with laughter, and then feel a little pang, because I love my wee sister and miss seeing her beaming smile in the mornings.

We amble along to the little craft shop at the Garrison. Aisha picks up a lemongrass candle and sticks it under my nose.

"Smell that, it's gorgeous. You could buy it for your mum."

"I'm a bit worried about it being a fire hazard. My mum wears a lot of floaty skirts and scarves. What if they catch fire when she's lighting her candle?"

"Lily, your mum is a grown woman. I'm sure she can cope with lighting a candle without you standing there with a fire extinguisher," laughs Aisha. "You need to stop being so responsible all the time. You're only eleven! Chill!"

I smile and buy the candle.

When we finish shopping, we spot the *Waverley* paddle steamer cruising by on its way to Rothesay. We run along the pier waving wildly at all the passengers. It's an impressive sight with its towering red and black funnels and gleaming paintwork.

"I'd like to steal the *Waverley* and sail away from here in it," says Aisha wistfully. "I'd travel right round the world. I'd go to Pakistan and find my dad."

"The only snag with that plan," I reply, "is that it doesn't have sails. The *Waverley*'s steam powered."

"Oh, crush my dreams, why don't you!" laughs Aisha, and she gives me a quick hug. I think we're good for each other, Aisha and me.

But the next day, it all goes a bit wrong.

On Wednesday afternoon, while we are sitting in the café sharing a knickerbocker glory, Aisha brings up the subject of going out on Imran's rowing boat. She starts to really push the idea hard.

"Please come, Lily," she moans. "Don't be a spoilsport. It's a lovely afternoon and the sea's flat calm. It won't be scary, I promise. You like bird watching, don't you? And there are grey seals on the rocks."

When I refuse, she gets quite annoyed with me.

"Why won't you, Lily? Is it because you haven't met my big brother yet? He's fine, honestly. Nothing like Aziz. Come and see!"

She grabs my hand and pulls me along the street. She doesn't listen to my protests that it wouldn't matter if her brother's an actual halo-wearing saint, I still don't want to go out in his boat. She pulls me through an open doorway and into a close. We head up the stairs to the first floor, where there is one highly-polished front door, with a brass letterbox. Aisha pushes open the door and yells.

"Mum! I've brought my friend Lily home, so she can inspect us. Come and say hello!"

A pleasant-looking lady, with eyes as dark as Aisha's and greying hair swept into a bun, comes out of the kitchen to welcome me. She is followed by a small boy of about seven who glowers when he sees us.

"Come in, Lily. Welcome!" smiles Aisha's mum and she guides me into the living room. It's a big, square room with high ceilings and one enormous bay window, with stunning views of the sea. There are squashy leather couches, a polished wood floor and thick woolly rugs.

There's a huge flat-screen television and even a piano. *This isn't the home of somebody poor*, I think, a little resentfully. It's nothing like my house.

Aziz pulls babyishly at his mum's skirt.

"Mum, I don't want Aisha's friend in my room," he whines.

"It's my room too, Aziz!" groans Aisha.

"But girls are smelly," he squeaks back.

"They don't smell nearly as badly as wee boys with mingin' socks and unwashed pants," says a gruff voice from behind us. "And you are the smelliest of the lot. Get lost, Aziz."

It's Imran and he is both funny and handsome, but I still don't want to go out to sea in his rowing boat. He looks like he should be in a boy band, with his short, glossy black hair, clear olive skin and long-lashed brown eyes.

He smiles politely as Aisha introduces us, and says that of course I'd be welcome to come out in *Seaspray*. I smile back just as politely and say that's very kind, but I would rather not. Aisha's face falls. She clearly thought that I would take one look at her gorgeous brother and change my mind.

"Why on earth are you making such a fuss, Lily?" she says, quite crossly. "It's a trip in a rowing boat, not a round-the-world cruise. We'd only be out at sea for a couple of hours."

"I'm just not keen on boats," I say lamely.

"You didn't have a problem coming over on the ferry," snaps Aisha.

Imran frowns at her and puts a warning hand on her shoulder. "Aisha, that's enough now. Lily said no. Leave it at that."

"Would you like to stay for dinner, Lily?" asks Aisha's mum.

"I'd love to, but my gran will have made my dinner by now. In fact, I'd better be getting home," I say hurriedly. "It was really nice to meet you all," I add, sticking my tongue out at Aziz as I turn to leave.

Aisha says nothing, and doesn't walk me to the door. She is clearly sulking and I hear Imran and her mother telling her off for her bad manners as I step out.

On Thursday it's so wet and stormy that I don't leave the caravan at all and spend the whole day playing cards and watching television with Gran.

"Are you all right, Lily?" she asks worriedly. "You're not bored?"

"No, this is fun. It feels like we're marooned in the middle of the ocean."

I'm lounging across the bench seats, head on a cushion,

listening to the howling wind and the crashing of the waves against the rocks. It feels really warm and cosy in the caravan. There's even a flame-effect electric fire.

"I hope we don't end up floating out to sea in this," says Gran, as the lights flicker and the caravan wobbles dramatically in the wind.

"Do you think that's possible?" I ask, suddenly anxious, sitting up and looking out at the crashing waves, imagining us suddenly being engulfed by a tsunami like you see on the news. My promise to the ghost suddenly seems a bit pointless if the sea is going to come and get me.

"No, this is just a summer storm," laughs Gran. "We'll not come to any harm, though I hope we don't get a power cut. I fancy another cup of tea."

Thankfully the power stays on and the sea stays where it should be. We have many more cups of tea and buttered toast and everything is fine.

I'm just hoping very much that the weather isn't like this tomorrow – falling out with Aisha has really made me miss Rowan and David.

Chapter 12

Things I love about this holiday:

- ★ Bacon and eggs for breakfast.
- ★ Cycling wherever I want.
- ★ Picnics on the beach at Fintry Bay.

Things I hate about this holiday:

- ★ Imran's stupid boat.
- ★ Scottish weather.
- ★ Ghostly nagging.

When I wake up on Friday morning, the first thing I do is throw back the duvet and pull the yellow curtains wide. The sun isn't shining. It's dull and cloudy, and disappointment shrouds me like fog. David and Rowan won't come if it stays like this.

I really want to see them. I miss them both. Aisha's great company (when she isn't in a sulk), but she is quite full on and that can be tiring. The time I spend with Rowan and David seems more relaxed, somehow. I know Rowan was angry with David and me when I last saw her, but I've never known her to stay angry.

Maybe I just haven't known Aisha long enough yet. Perhaps our friendship will grow stronger; or perhaps, I think sadly, it's all over already if she hasn't forgiven me for refusing to come out in her brother's stupid rowing boat.

"Lily, your bacon's burning!" shouts Gran and I hurry through to the living area, where Gran is standing over the tiny hob, cooking bacon and eggs in a pan.

"There you are at last," she says, scooping two rashers and a fried egg on to a plate. "Eat up. You're far too much of a skinnymalink."

"Thanks Gran," I say gratefully, feeling a bit sad that I'll be home soon, and will have to make my own breakfast in the morning if I want to eat. Mum doesn't usually bother with cooked breakfasts, and sometimes the milk is sour and the bread is stale.

"Does your mother make you breakfast?" asks Gran suddenly, her sharp eyes boring into me. I wonder if she just read my thoughts. "Sometimes I think those wee ones are famished when they arrive at my door in the mornings."

There's no way I'm going to tell Gran the truth. It's not that I get some kick out of telling lies, like Aisha seems to, but I don't want Gran to think less of my mum than she does already.

"We usually have cereal and toast, Gran, not big fry ups," I tell her. "And sometimes we have beans or scrambled eggs on toast." That's not a real lie, as we have had beans and toast for dinner lots of times this year, just not for breakfast.

I slide along the bench with my plate and sit down at the table, looking out the window at the leaden sky and the frothing, foam-flecked waves.

Gran notices my scowling face and reads my mind for the second time this morning.

"Don't worry about that grey sky," she says briskly. "The forecast is for sunshine in the afternoon. The woman on the radio says that it's to get quite hot, though that's hard to believe looking at those rain clouds. If the sun does come out, I'm going to sit outside on my chair and sunbathe with a magazine and cups of tea. Are you going to join me or have you got plans for the day?"

I beam delightedly. I suddenly have lots of plans.

"I'm going to head into Millport and hang around there in case Rowan and David come after school ends at twelve," I say. "And if they don't make it, Aisha and I might walk up to the viewpoint and have a picnic. We can buy sandwiches in the wee supermarket."

Gran nods happily. She seems really pleased that I am having such a great holiday, and probably equally pleased that I am leaving her in peace to enjoy herself in her own way. Poor Gran spends such a lot of her time running about after all of us. I'm glad she is getting time to relax, for a change.

After a lazy morning chatting with Gran and writing in my journal, the weather is looking more promising. I put on my skinny jeans, my orange shoes and a grey t-shirt with TEE embroidered on the front in white.

"I wish that Rowan and Dave will make it over here today," I whisper as I remove my water lily charm from my backpack and put it on the zip of my jeans. Maybe it will bring me luck.

I look at myself in the small mirror and am glad I ventured to the dreaded shower block during last night's storm, as my hair looks good. The sun has lightened it, so it's almost as if I've got highlights.

"Hurry along, Lily. Stop admiring yourself and get out in the fresh air. You're wasting the last day of your holidays!" shouts Gran.

I wave goodbye to her and grab the bike. Tomorrow my precious bike is going back to its rightful owners, and I am dreading losing the freedom it has given me. I whizz along the single-track road, tyres scrunching on the gravel, and head towards the town. Wet brown seaweed, bleached driftwood and the odd plastic bottle are scattered on the shoreline, blown in on last night's storm.

When I get to Millport, I cycle up and down the length of the promenade, scanning the street and the beach. I get off the bike and walk along the pavement, looking in all the shop and café windows, just in case Rowan and David have somehow arrived early.

I feel like I must be the only eleven-year-old girl in the world who doesn't own a mobile phone, although phone reception is a bit iffy on the island anyway, so I could easily miss a text or phone call. Still, not having a phone makes me feel different from everyone else and I already stand out enough as it is. Maybe I can talk Gran into getting me one when I start secondary. I could tell her it would be useful in emergencies. It wouldn't be a lie.

When I pass the Wedge, Aisha crosses my mind. It's the end of term for her too and I wonder what she's doing. I consider going up and knocking on her door, but I'm a bit nervous in case she's still cross with me. I decide that if I go right to the end of the town and back, and Rowan and David still haven't appeared, then I'll go up and see her and hope that she's in a better mood.

As I wander past the Garrison, a red Citroën slows down and two people leap out of the back seat.

"Hi, Lily! We made it!" shouts David. They're here!

Rowan's mum is driving the car and their bikes are strapped on a rack at the back.

"Oh, this is great!" I say, leaning my bike against the Garrison wall and hugging them delightedly.

"My mum was dead against the whole idea yesterday but then, when she saw the forecast this morning, she changed her mind and said she would take us over on the ferry straight from school," explains Rowan. "She's going to meet up with some friends who have a holiday flat here."

"I was gutted when I got up and saw all those clouds," David laughs. "But it's brightening up already. We're going to have a brilliant day!"

I am totally thrilled to see my best friends and give them both another hug. It looks like Rowan has forgiven us.

"Are you having a good holiday?" asks Rowan. "Or have you been missing us too much?"

"I'm having a fun time," I answer truthfully. "But it's even better now that you two are here."

I help them unstrap their bikes while Rowan's mum fusses over the details.

"Don't forget to meet me at seven o'clock outside the Garrison, Rowan. I'm going out with your father tonight and we *must* get the half-seven ferry home."

"No problem, Mrs Forrest," says David, smiling sweetly. "We've got our mobiles so we will keep a good eye on the time."

David has a real talent for dealing with difficult adults.

"And be careful on those bicycles. Wear your helmets. And use the suntan lotion that I've put in the picnic bag," she witters on. "And take care when you're crossing roads!"

I think worriedly that the day will be over before Mrs Forrest stops giving out safety instructions, but she eventually runs out of ways we could injure or kill ourselves. We wave goodbye and walk with the bikes across the street to the long promenade.

"I've got picnic stuff in my backpack," says Rowan excitedly. "We've got ham and cheese sandwiches and hummus and breadsticks. The hummus was my mum's idea – we can feed it to the seagulls. And there's iced ginger cake, cans of coke and grapes."

"Let's head for Fintry Bay and eat. I'm ravenous," says David, who's always ravenous.

We cycle up the hill, past the park and out of the town. Then we get off the bikes and walk for a bit so that we can chat. I ask them to tell me all about the last week of school.

"The dance was great," says Rowan, at exactly the same time as David says:

"The dance was a nightmare."

"So which was it?" I laugh. "There seems to be a difference of opinion here."

"Rowan looked very pretty in her *Little Mermaid* dress.

And she knows all the steps of the 'Dashing White Sergeant' and 'Strip the Willow', so she had a great time" sighs David. "I looked a total dork in my ridiculous kilt and I have two left feet, so I loathed every minute. No, make that every second. The minutes were endless."

"It was really good fun, Lily," says Rowan. "We sang Auld Lang Syne at the end in a big circle."

"Did Mrs McKenzie join in?" I ask. It seems as unthinkable as the Queen doing karaoke.

"Yep," says Rowan. "She danced nearly all night. Did I not see her dancing with you a couple of times, David?"

"That was so I wasn't left sitting on my own at the edge of the dance floor like a sad wallflower," sighs David. "Though I think I preferred being Nigel-no-mates. Mrs McKenzie kept standing on my toes."

"Doug the Thug was dead cool in his kilt. He looked like a Celtic warrior out of *Braveheart*," says Rowan. "All the girls were amazed by how well he scrubbed up. You might have fancied him, Lily."

"I think not," I reply. "If I ever decide I want to go out with a boy, the ability to speak in words of more than one syllable will be the deciding factor, not whether or not he looks handsome in a kilt."

"I thought he looked pretty good," says David thoughtfully, and Rowan and I glance at each other and grin.

"What about yesterday's end-of-term service?" I ask. "Was that a real schmaltz-fest?"

"It was lovely," says Rowan wistfully. "Some of the parents were actually crying when we sang 'Child of Tomorrow'."

"That might have been because Mrs McKenzie had just made a speech about how we will be teenagers soon," says David. "Parents never want to hear that. They were genuinely distressed."

"David made a lovely wee speech," breaks in Rowan. "He said that Mrs McKenzie had inspired him to work hard and to follow his dreams of being a film director one day. She got quite tearful too."

"It only seemed lovely," retorts David, "because it followed Big Cheryl's unscripted number about how she hated primary school and couldn't wait to see the back of it."

"Oh, you should have seen Mrs McKenzie's face during Cheryl's speech," says Rowan. "If I'd been Cheryl, I would have been very afraid. Mrs McKenzie was giving her the demon glare."

"Lily's never seen Mrs McKenzie's demon glare, Rowan," laughs David. "She's far too much of a teacher's pet."

I listen to my friends batting their words back and forth. I am starting to feel a little twinge of excitement about starting secondary school, replacing the dread. It won't be so bad if I have Rowan and David with me. I feel suddenly more confident that we will all stay friends forever, and hopeful that Rowan still cares more about me and David than she does about her netball girls.

And it's not a bad thing if we all make new friends too. Friends like Aisha, hopefully.

"I've gotten to know a girl here on Millport who'll be at secondary school with us in August," I say. "Her name's Aisha and she's good fun. Do you want to meet up with her later?"

"Sure, that'll be good," they say. "What's she like?"

We get back on the bikes and cycle on towards Fintry Bay while I try and describe Aisha.

The picnic is delicious, especially the iced ginger cake. David throws some hummus at a lurking seagull, but it turns up its beak.

"No wonder, the stuff looks like cat sick," I say.

After lunch, we sunbathe on the beach. The sun has come out, just as Gran said it would, and it's a glorious day. I borrow some of Rowan's suntan lotion and slap it on. People with ginger hair and pale skin should never venture out in the sun without taking major protective measures. I've learned that the hard way.

Rowan even goes in for a wee paddle, but sees a jellyfish, and splashes out of the water screaming as though she'd just spotted a great white shark.

We explore the rocky foreshore and Rowan and David are quite impressed that I know my curlews from my oystercatchers and my cormorants from my gannets. I scan the shoreline, hoping to be able to show them a leaping porpoise or the fin of a basking shark, though remembering Rowan's hysterics over the jellyfish, perhaps that wouldn't be a good plan.

In the middle of the afternoon we head back into town and mooch about the shops for a little while. David is entranced to find Star Wars figures in the toy shop and we have trouble dragging him back out into the sunshine.

I show them where Aisha lives and we are about to head up to her flat, when she appears in the doorway. Maybe she has been watching from her window, because it seems quite a coincidence. She looks enchanting in a short green summer dress and soft leather sandals.

She rushes over and greets me warmly, Wednesday's quarrel seemingly forgotten.

I introduce Rowan and David and they all grin at each other, a bit awkwardly.

"What are your plans now?" asks Aisha. "Are you going to cycle round the island? I believe it's compulsory for day-trippers. If you haven't been round at least once, they won't let you on the return ferry."

Rowan laughs and I can see she is falling for Aisha's charm. I feel proud that I met her first.

"We've already cycled to Fintry Bay," says Rowan. "I don't know if I'm up for another bike ride already. You're a local. What are Millport's hottest attractions? Besides the rock that has been painted to look vaguely like a crocodile, I mean. That's a bit desperate."

"There's the Lion Rock and the Indian Rock too," I laugh. "We could do a Rock Tour."

"My brother's got a wee boat," says Aisha, coolly. "We could ask him to take us out in it. It's only a rowing boat but it should get us out as far as Little Cumbrae. There are seals and they're so cute."

I try and glare at her, but she isn't looking my way. She has Rowan and David in her sights and delivers a killer shot.

"Imran was out in the boat last weekend and he was followed around by a young dolphin that just wanted to play, and was leaping in front of the boat. He said it was the most amazing thing ever."

I can't believe I'm hearing this. She knows I don't want to go on the boat. Ok, I haven't given her much of a reason, but I've said no several times. I glare again, but Aisha is avoiding my eyes.

Rowan and Dave have no idea that I have vetoed the whole boat thing and think it's a brilliant idea. When they see Imran, I know they will be even more convinced.

"I'll go up and ask him," says Aisha, still not looking at me. "I'm sure it will be ok. He said earlier he'd like to take the boat out now it's such a lovely day."

I open my mouth to say I don't want to go, but I'm still trying to come up with the words when Aisha runs off into her close, and Rowan and David both turn towards me, beaming.

"This is going to be so good," grins David. "I've always wanted to see dolphins in the wild. I saw them in a marine park when Mum took me to the Netherlands last Easter, but that's not the same at all."

"Aisha's great," says Rowan enthusiastically. "She's fun and she's so pretty too, isn't she?"

I look down at the ground, at the dried blobs of chewing gum on the pavement. I don't want to talk about Aisha. I'm angry with her for forcing me into this situation and I'm trying to figure out what to do. Should I go on the stupid rowing boat and break my promise to the ghost? I was so looking forward to spending time with my friends, and how dangerous can a little boat be on a day like today? But if the ghost's right, it could be the last thing I ever do.

David doesn't answer Rowan either. He is watching as Aisha runs back down her stairway, closely followed by

Imran, tall and impossibly gorgeous in blue jeans and a white t-shirt.

"Hi, landlubbers," says Imran, grinning at us. "I'll take you down to the jetty and we'll have a quick row round the bay in *Seaspray*. I don't start work 'til seven o'clock, so we should have three or so hours out there. I warn you though, when we get out of the shelter of the bay, the water can be quite choppy."

"No problem, I've rowed on the Largs boating pond. Can't be scarier than that," says David.

We cross the road, pushing the bikes, and Imran strides ahead towards the jetty. I can see his little rowing boat tied up there, painted in blue and white stripes, with '*Seaspray*' carefully written on the hull.

Imran jumps aboard and Aisha leaps in after him. The boat rocks wildly and I know without a doubt that I can't go out to sea with them, however much I wish I could. Rowan and David clamber into the boat and it rocks to and fro again. The movement makes me feel cold and seasick and I'm still on the jetty.

"May the Force be with us!" yells David cheerfully.

"It's a rowing boat, you eejit, not a spaceship," laughs Rowan.

They don't have a clue how I'm feeling.

Imran holds out his hand, and I step back so quickly that I stumble.

"I'm sorry," I mutter. "I don't want to come. I'm just going to stay here and wait for you. It's not a problem."

"Aw, come on Lil!" shouts David, in surprise. "It'll be fun. Come with us, please. Don't be daft!"

I look at his shocked face, and suddenly feel panicky. What if something awful happens to my friends? Maybe they should be staying away from boats too.

"Please don't go," I say desperately. "I don't want you to go out in a boat. It might… it might capsize or something. You might drown. You're not wearing life jackets. Shouldn't you have life jackets?"

Rowan looks anxious and upset, while Aisha just looks irritated. "Lily, you really need to chill. Stop thinking that everything is a disaster waiting to happen!"

"I'm not going without Lily," Rowan says, trying to stand up and causing the boat to wobble dangerously.

"Don't worry, Imran knows what he's doing," says Aisha firmly. "We'll be back in no time! If Lily really isn't keen, she can entertain herself for a bit and meet us after. Can't you, Lily?"

"Sure," I say, trying hard to smile and look relaxed. "Course I can. Sit down, Rowan, before you fall in! Have a good time. I'll see you all soon."

There's no way I can convince them that I'm genuinely worried without having to explain that I'm being pestered by an angsty, insistent ghost telling me over and over again not to go near water.

I turn and stride down the jetty, doing my best to hold my head high. I can hear the splashing of oars, and a shriek of laughter from Aisha. They are going without me.

Chapter 13

Things I'm surprised about:

⭐ When I'm really upset, I sulk like Jenna.
⭐ Marshmallow ice cream can't fix everything.
⭐ I may not survive this holiday.

For a while I cycle round and round Millport, in fast furious circuits, until my legs are aching and I am gasping with thirst. Then I go and sit in the Ritz café for nearly an hour, hunched moodily among all the loud day-trippers, with their screaming toddlers and whining children. I stick coins in the jukebox and put on all the saddest songs I can find. I order a coke and a marshmallow ice cream with raspberry sauce. The ice cream tastes delicious, but it isn't making me any happier. I remember that I haven't bought Jenna a present yet and wander around the gift shops, but I can't see anything she'd like. Perhaps I'll give her my water lily charm. It's not bringing me much luck.

I am worried sick, and sick of my own company. But I am also fizzing with rage. Why did Aisha have to go on about Imran's boat when she *knew* I didn't want to go out in it? I couldn't have made it any clearer, could I?

And why did Rowan and Dave agree so readily to go with her when this is supposed to be our day out together? They are totally disloyal and I feel betrayed by them all. I wish bitterly that I had never met Aisha. She has stolen my friends. She has ruined my holiday.

"It's not fair!" I grumble, kicking out at a railing, and then feel instantly embarrassed. I'm acting like Jenna in a strop, or the boys in mid-tantrum.

"Grow up!" I hiss furiously at myself. "Act your age, not your shoe size."

I look out to sea and see the little boat bobbing far off in the water, its colours blending in with the sea foam and sky. It looks very small and fragile. What if something awful does happen to them all? I should have tried harder to stop them. I close my eyes, imagining the boat capsizing, imagining my friends being thrown into the choppy, grey water. It's a horrible prospect… but it isn't very likely to happen, is it? It's the Firth of Clyde, not the Atlantic Ocean.

Maybe Aisha is right and I need to stop thinking that

disaster is lurking around every corner. I should be out there in that boat, having a lovely time with my friends. And I would have gone, if it wasn't for that ghostly girl, tormenting me with her gloomy warnings.

I cycle down Stuart Street towards the old pier and the George Hotel. When I get to the little harbour, I stop and dump my bike against the sea wall. The tide is low and so the slope leading down to the harbour is dry. I sit there on the stones, away from the busy street and the crowds of noisy day-trippers. The harbour smells of seaweed and engine oil.

An enormous grey gull waddles over to see what it can steal, and for some reason this is the final straw. My anger boils over.

"Get lost," I shout fiercely, flapping my arms to make it go away.

"There's no need to be so horrible!" says an affronted voice. "I'm only trying to help you – to help us!"

I turn and see my ghost sitting on the harbour wall. I scramble to my feet and go and sit by her side. She no longer frightens me at all.

I can see her quite clearly now, as if she is a photo on a computer screen which has been rendering before coming suddenly into focus. Now that she has more colour, I can see that she has gingery hair and pale, freckled skin. Her eyes are as wide and grey as they always were. She is wearing shorts, and a t-shirt with Hello Kitty printed on the front, and she is clutching a tatty, stuffed toy lion with a pink fluorescent mane tightly in her arms.

I know her now.

"Summer?" I whisper, my voice trembling.

She nods sadly, reaches out a hand and strokes my face, but I can't feel it. She has no substance at all. My little sister is my ghost but she's not from the past at all. She's from the future. I can't process this.

"What's going on?" I say desperately. "What are you doing here, Summer?"

"Mum didn't get over losing you," she says.

I go cold. What is she talking about? Nobody has lost me. I'm not even mislaid. I'm with Gran, on holiday in Millport. I'm having a bad day, that's all.

"She didn't cope at all and Gran was no better. Gran blamed herself and had to move away—"

"Blamed herself for what?" I interrupt, a bit rudely, but I'm really anxious to understand what exactly is going on here.

Summer's voice sounds a bit like Mum's, a little like Jenna's, probably like mine, too. No wonder it seemed so familiar.

"She blamed herself for your accident, of course. She was in charge of you, and you died. Mum didn't manage without her once she moved, of course."

"Hold on, hold on," I stutter. "I actually died? I'm going to die?" I shake my head dumbly.

"Nobody ever talked about it in detail, but I know you drowned on holiday when I was two..." she says sadly. "That's when everything started to go wrong."

There's one question I'm desperate to ask, but I'm almost too afraid to say it.

"Are you a ghost?" I stammer.

"What? No, I'm not dead! I told you before."

I'm so relieved I could laugh, despite all the worries and questions whizzing round my head.

"But things are bad, Lily," she continues, "after Gran left, our wee family fell apart." I imagine all the food emergencies, the failed appointments, the unsigned permission slips, the unwashed laundry. "Jenna went completely off the rails. I don't know where she ended up – Mum kicked her out when I was four. I'm sorry, Lily. I hardly remember her."

I want to cry, thinking of how sad and scared Jenna must have been, being told to leave her own home. Jenna can't help being angry. Mum should realise that she's responsible for some of it by bringing that awful man into our lives, I think furiously. I promise myself I'll be kinder to Jenna, if I make it off this island alive.

I take some deep breaths to calm my thudding heart, and remind myself that this hasn't happened yet. It's all in the future. Right now, Jenna and baby Summer are at home with Mum and the boys. Everybody is fine. I just need to change the future, so that these horrible things don't happen. It can't be that difficult, surely. Can it?

"What about the wee boys?" I ask, torn between needing to know and not wanting to know.

"Bronx and Hudson are in all kinds of trouble with the police," says Summer, looking as if she's afraid to tell me such bad news. Does she think I don't know them? Without Gran and me bossing the boys around and keeping them in order, they'd run wild, like little feral cats.

"Bronx is in a Young Offenders Unit at the moment. Hudson drinks too much. He copies Dad."

"Dad?" I shout the word and it echoes off the harbour wall. Surely she doesn't mean my step-dad. Does a restraining order not count for anything these days?

"Dad came back into our lives when I was about five. Mum needed help. But he just made everything so much worse."

I feel suddenly furious with Mum. How could she have let that happen? She promised we would never have to see that man again. I can imagine, though, that if my mum was desperately unhappy and lonely without Gran, Jenna and me, he would have been able to worm his way back into her life.

"He scares me when he's drunk," Summer whispers. "He shouts and falls and breaks things."

Summer's face is clouded in misery and I can't bear to think about her having a dreadful, neglected childhood. I think of my baby sister's cheerful grin every time I lift her out of that awful playpen. I think of her waving her cute little chubby hands as I wheel her along the sea front.

She doesn't deserve a future like the one she's describing, and neither do my little brothers, or my big sister.

Summer wraps her arms tightly around the scruffy little lion. "I only know that if you hadn't died, everything would have been different. Mum says that you were the only one who really had any time for me. You gave me Roary. I need to save you. I've been trying to warn you. It's just really difficult to get noticed.

"How..." I croak, still unable to deal with all this information. "How are you doing this?"

She hugs the lion close to her chest. I feel oddly pleased that it means so much to her. The animal really is in the most awful state: filthy, with mangy orange fur, one plastic eye and a threadbare pink mane.

"Since I turned eleven, the age you were when you died, when I hold Roary really tightly like this, and close my eyes, and think about how I felt when you first gave him to me, somehow I'm able to communicate with you," she explains. "At first I wasn't sure if you could hear or see me. I even thought that I was just imagining you, because I was wishing so hard that you hadn't drowned. But then you started answering me back. Once I realised what was happening, I did everything I could to warn you… though you weren't very friendly," she adds, a bit crossly.

"Well I couldn't see you at first, could I? You have no idea how creepy it is to be spoken to by a disembodied voice. And when you started to become visible, you were so faint that I thought you were a ghost."

Everything that has happened over the last few weeks begins to make sense. Why I recognised her but didn't recognise her, why she changed her clothes, why she was as confused and surprised as I was to be crossing through time and space to talk to me.

"Summer, you need to tell me what happens to me so I can stop it."

Summer grips Roary tightly. Tears fill her large grey eyes. "All I know is that you drowned on holiday on June 26th. Mum loses it every year on that day. So I have been trying to change our future by changing your past. I have no idea if that's possible, Lily."

It had better be possible, I think furiously. I have no intention of drowning this week or any other. The 26th is today, and I already chose not to go on the boat. All I have to do is get through today and everything and everybody will be ok.

But what if the boat sinks whether I'm on it or not? My friends are still out on the choppy water!

"What about my friends?" I blurt out. "Was it just me who died?"

"I'm sorry Lily, I don't know," she sighs. "Like I said, nobody ever talks to me about it."

I should have pleaded with them to stay on dry land. I should have told them why I was so reluctant to go on the boat. I picture police and search helicopters, and Mrs Forrest's face when I have to tell her I let them get on a boat without life jackets on. I feel sick with fear and panic, but upsetting Summer even more isn't going to help any of us.

"Well," I say as calmly and as big-sisterly as I'm able, "I'm not dead and I've no plans to die just yet. By tomorrow I'll be back in Largs and I promise I'll take good care of you all and be the best big sister ever. I'll even forgive you for haunting me."

I can't believe I'm looking at my brave, grown-up little sister. I reach out to give her a hug, forgetting that she is as insubstantial as mist. She looks at me with her wide, sad eyes and then as I watch, she fizzles, colours dissolving, like a popping bubble. I am sitting on the wall by myself.

The June sun is still bright although it's nearly evening. I stay on the wall in the sunshine and try to sort out my jumble of thoughts. Maybe this is just a particularly weird nightmare and I will wake up in the caravan and Gran will be frying sausages for breakfast and nobody will be talking about death, except maybe Gran, as its one of her favourite subjects.

But all of this is real. Too real. And the little boat containing my best friends in the world is nowhere to be seen.

Chapter 14

Ways to avoid disaster:

★ Don't hurt people's feelings.
★ Don't sneak out in the night.
★ Always listen to warnings, particularly when people have travelled through time to give them. Why would they go to all that bother, if they weren't deadly serious?

I stand up on the wall, heart racing, scanning the horizon for any signs of Imran's boat. Disasters do happen – Summer's sad story has convinced me of that. I don't want any of the people I love to come to any harm, just as much as I don't want anything bad to happen to me. And I still can't see the boat. What if it's been smashed to smithereens against the rocks…? What if my friends are clinging helplessly to the wreckage, slipping under the waves...?

Panicking, I hurry over to the jetty where the bikes are still lying abandoned. Where are they? Should I call the police? The coastguard?

Suddenly, with a shudder of relief, I can make out the tiny striped boat heading towards the jetty. Imran is rowing and the rest are laughing at Aisha, who is standing up in the boat, shrieking and waving at me excitedly. She looks like a pretty elf with her short black hair and green summer dress.

My fear dissolves, but it turns out my anger was clinging underneath it like a fog.

"Show off," I murmur bitterly, but I fix a smile on my face.

I keep smiling while Imran ties up the boat and the others run over. David's hair is more unruly than ever and his neck is sunburnt. He looks happy and excited.

"Hi, guys," I say, as casually as I can. "Did you have a good time?"

I am unbelievably happy to see them all in one piece, but I am still so angry with Aisha, I can hardly look at her.

"It was really good," enthuses David. "Imran rowed right out to Little Cumbrae! I saw three grey seals sunbathing on the rocks. It was amazing! We didn't see any dolphins, but Imran says if we're here again later in the summer he might take us out for another look."

"David and Rowan did some of the rowing," added Aisha, her big brown eyes bright with excitement. "But every time I tried, the boat went round in circles. I was the world's worst!"

"The seals were fantastic. They have gorgeous big soppy eyes," said Rowan. "But there were some big waves once we rowed out of the bay. It was quite choppy! I felt a bit seasick. And I was sad you weren't with us, Lily."

"Yeah, it wasn't the same without you. I wish you'd come too," added David.

I shrug, pretending I don't care.

"I didn't fancy it, guys," I say truthfully. "I felt seasick just looking at the boat bobbing on the water."

"I'm starving! Is anyone else hungry? Will we get fish and chips?" asks Aisha.

I turn my back on her, quite deliberately, still seething with anger.

"What time is it?" asks Rowan. "We said we would meet Mum outside the Garrison at seven o'clock."

"It's nearly seven," I say dully. "You'd better go and meet her."

I feel horrible. Sulky and bad tempered. I don't like the way I sound or the way I'm behaving, but I'm having trouble snapping out of it. While some of it is to do with feeling left out, I'm also still brimming with anger and distress over everything Summer told me about my family's future without me.

"Are you ok, Lily?" asks David, looking at me seriously over the rims of his round glasses. "You don't look happy."

I bite my lip, to stop myself from bursting into silly tears, and give myself a mental shake. After all, I reason, it was my choice not to go on the boat trip. It wasn't as if they were deliberately excluding me. I pride myself on being mature and now I'm behaving like a babyish eejit.

Grow up Lily, you're not two years old, I think crossly, and am reminded instantly of wee Summer. Maybe if I'd gone with my friends in that rickety little rowing boat, I'd have fallen out and drowned. Maybe the boat would've been overcrowded and we'd have *all* drowned. Summer and I might have actually just managed to change all of our futures!

This thought cheers me up so much that I'm able to smile easily back at David.

"I'm fine, really," I say. "I just felt a bit sad because it's time for you to go home and I would have liked you to stay longer."

Rowan, David, Aisha and I are pushing our bikes towards the Garrison when the red Citroën draws up beside us and Rowan's mum sticks her head out of the window.

"Hi kids. Have you had a good day? Are you ready to go?"

As she speaks, I realise how much I don't want my

friends to leave. I thought I might have lost them forever and I've just got them back. And I don't want to be alone tonight, worrying. I am determined to do something to fix this day. I can do anything, even alter the future.

"'Scuse me, Mrs Forrest," I say hurriedly, rushing up to the car window. "My gran and I were wondering if Rowan and David would like to stay the night and come back with us tomorrow."

It is such a spectacular fib that I can't believe it's coming out of my mouth. Mrs Forrest looks very doubtful. She doesn't even let her daughter come round to my house. Why did I think she would let Rowan stay the night with me? The only positive thing is that she has met my gran quite often at the school gate and at sports days and stuff and knows that she's the kind of lady who won't stand for any nonsense. For once my gran being a bossy mare might work in my favour.

Rowan and David are so excited at the prospect that they are actually jumping up and down on the pavement.

"Oh go on, Mum!" shrieks Rowan. "It'll be brilliant. I've never stayed in a caravan before."

"You don't have spare clothes or a toothbrush, Rowan," says Mrs Forrest.

"I'll be home in the morning, Mum," wheedles Rowan. "It won't kill me to wear the same underwear two days in a row and my teeth will survive until tomorrow."

I wonder if Rowan should cry. That usually helps her to get her own way. I wish her dad was here. We need somebody who crumbles quickly under pressure!

"Well, let me phone David's mother and make sure it's all right with her first, and then I will call Lily's gran."

I shake my head. Gran will have a pink fit if the campsite owners come round to tell her she has a phone call.

"There's no phone reception at the campsite at all," I say, thinking on my feet. "But I asked Gran earlier today and she says it's totally fine. It's a lovely big three-bedroom caravan. There's loads of room. Gran says she will bring us all home on the ferry first thing tomorrow morning."

I am determined that this lie is going to work out, that my lovely day with my friends can still be salvaged, and that I will not be alone, thoroughly spooked by the day's events, tonight. I'm not one bit sure about how my gran will react, but I will cross that bridge when I come to it.

Mrs Forrest has an unnecessarily long conversation on the phone with David's mum while we hop excitedly about on the pavement. I am planning in my head what we can do tonight, the three of us.

Aisha is not included in my plans at all.

Eventually, Rowan's mum ends her call and lets us know the verdict.

"Sandra thinks that it's a very kind offer, as long as you are sure it is fine with your grandmother."

"Oh, it's absolutely, definitely fine with her," I insist, hoping against hope that I'm telling the truth.

Rowan's mum gives her a hug.

"Be good," she says, still looking a little anxious. "You'll need to ride your bikes round to the ferry in the morning by yourselves. Will you manage that?"

"Mum, we're not babies," groans Rowan. "We'll be totally fine."

"Well, I want you all to cycle straight over to the campsite right now, do you hear? You've not to wander around the town at night without an adult. Are you listening?"

We all agree that we will go to the campsite, just as soon as we've had some chips, and we wave cheerfully as Rowan's mum drives off to catch the half-past-seven ferry.

Aisha suddenly announces that she needs to get home. I wave a casual hand in her direction, hardly acknowledging her. Rowan and David are more polite, and thank her for the boat trip, and ask if she is sure she doesn't want to get fish and chips, after all. But I think Aisha has finally realised that I am freezing her out, and she turns her bike and walks quietly away.

As soon as I see her leaving, I feel major pangs of guilt. I am being really mean to her, and it's not like me to be mean. I'm about to call her back, but can't think what to say, so I let her go.

Rowan, David and I go to the chip shop, buy three fish suppers and eat them sitting on a bench at the old pier. I am getting butterflies thinking of bringing my two uninvited guests back to Gran's caravan. She can be very forthright, my gran.

"Come on Lil," says Rowan, scrunching up the greasy paper and flinging it in the bin. "Let's go and see this caravan."

We cycle home in the evening sunshine. It's a beautiful night, still warm even at nearly eight o'clock. We stop for a rest at the war memorial and watch a hedgehog amble down the little path towards the beach. It senses our presence and freezes, its nose twitching comically.

"It must think that if it keeps really still, we can't see it," laughs Rowan.

With my best friends happily chatting away either side of me, I think about what a good job Summer has done warning me, even if it was very scary and unsettling at first. I feel weirdly proud of her, and reasonably hopeful that she has saved my life. Now all I have to do when I get home is make sure I return the favour, and give her a better, happier future.

And I realise that even though I was stressed, I did manage to stand up for myself. I didn't let Aisha force me into going out on her brother's boat. I didn't feel safe and I said no. Right now I'm pretty glad about that.

As we approach the caravan site, I start having serious doubts. What if Gran tells them to go home? I will die of shame. But I underestimate her. Again.

"Hi Gran," I call, as I see her still sitting outside in the sunshine, squeezed into her folding chair, which looks as if it might collapse under her weight at any second.

"I've brought Rowan and David to see the caravan. Rowan's mum says it's ok for them to stay the night." I look pleadingly at Gran as I speak, hoping against hope that she won't embarrass me. But her face breaks into a big smile.

"How lovely that your friends can stay over!" she says cheerfully, "Have you eaten? Would you like bacon rolls?"

David would, despite having demolished a fish supper only half an hour ago.

We sit on a rug in the evening sunshine, drinking hot chocolate that Gran makes for us. Then, when the midges start to bite, we head indoors and sit round the table playing Cluedo and cards. At ten o'clock Gran announces that she's heading for bed and she shows David where he'll be sleeping, in the smaller bunk room. Rowan is sharing with me, and for once I have no objections to sharing my room.

But I don't want this evening to end, and I'm still freaked out about being alone with my thoughts if Rowan falls asleep quickly. When I hear Gran's snores echoing around the caravan, I turn to Rowan and David.

"Do you fancy heading into Millport on our bikes?" I ask, thinking that tonight I'm behaving more like reckless Aisha than my usual sensible self. Their surprised expressions confirm this, so I quickly revert to type. I can't help myself.

"The bikes all have lights so it won't be dangerous," I say, doing a quick risk assessment in my head. "There won't be any traffic on the roads either."

Rowan and David agree that this is a great plan and we sneak stealthily out of the front door, leaving my gran sleeping alone in the caravan. We almost trip over our bikes, abandoned on the grass, and Rowan has a fit of giggles.

"Shh!" hisses David, as a dog starts to bark in a nearby caravan. "You'd make a useless burglar, Row."

Cumbrae seems very different in the moonlight. Coloured lights from across the water twinkle in the distance and are reflected in the black water. A tawny owl hoots eerily. A tiny mouse scurries along the grass verge. It's all a bit spooky.

"I hope we don't bump into any ghostly apparitions in the dark," says David. I hope so too, but for different reasons. I'm hoping Summer is living happily in the future.

The journey seems to take much longer than usual and I'm chilly, despite Jenna's fluffy pink cardigan. I am beginning to regret the whole stupid plan, but then see Millport's streetlights glowing ahead. We've made it!

The streets of the town are deserted, though we can hear loud, tuneless singing echoing from the George Hotel. It must be karaoke night, or that daft guy serenading the girl from the kitchens.

"What do we do now?" asks Rowan. It's a good question. The beach is dark and uninviting and the shops and cafés are long closed. A police car is driving slowly down the main street and we turn into a side road to avoid them. Gran will kill me if we are brought home by the police. This was a bad idea.

We are circling round the harbour area a bit aimlessly when I catch sight of a small figure sitting forlornly at the edge of the pier. For a minute I think it must be Summer. I'm instantly afraid that I haven't changed the future after all, and that my life is still in danger.

But then I realise that it's Aisha sitting there, head bowed in the semi-darkness. I shout to David and Rowan to wait for me for a moment and cycle over to where she is perched, legs dangling over the water.

"Aisha?" I call and she jumps in alarm.

"I diagnose an overactive startle response." I say jokily, but then I see she is in no mood for joking. Her eyes are full of tears. I feel instantly responsible. I should have invited her to stay overnight too.

"Go away," she sobs. "You made it quite clear that we're not friends any more."

"I was angry about the boat, Aisha," I explain. "I'd told you loads of times that I didn't want to go."

"I hoped you'd change your mind when you saw your friends wanted to come."

"I had good reasons, Aisha, and if you are going to be my friend, you'll need to accept that if I say 'no', I mean it. It's not nice to force anyone, or guilt anyone, into doing things they don't want to do." Making my feelings clear is not something I'm usually good at and I'm quite surprised and pleased that I've managed to assert myself like this. But I know I have to say more, in order to make things better between us. I'm in the wrong here too. "But Aisha, that doesn't excuse how rude and mean to you I was when you came back from the boat and I'm very sorry about that. Can we call it quits and start again?"

Aisha looks up at me, her face crumpled with grief.

"I don't have any friends left at school," she says in a tiny voice. "Imran gave me a massive talking to this evening. He says I need to calm down and stop showing off or I won't make friends in secondary school either. He says that I was showing off so much in the boat that it almost capsized and I put everyone in danger."

I can't believe what I'm hearing. I think of the little boat rocking to and fro, precariously low in the water. Any extra weight and the boat could have tipped right over. And there were no life jackets. I send out a huge, silent thank you to Summer.

Aisha, though, is still in despair. "I think I must be a horrible person, Lily. Do you think that's why my dad left? Was it because he thought I was a liar and a show-off too?"

"No, Aisha, of course it wasn't why he left. You're not a horrible person. You're just a bit mixed up and upset right now. I bet your dad loves you to bits. Whatever's going on with him, it will have nothing to do with you. Honestly, I mean it."

Aisha's brown eyes are brimming with tears.

"Really, Lily? You don't think Dad left because of me?"

I step forward, planning to give her one of my awkward pats on the back, when I trip clumsily on one of the heavy iron rings bolted to the pier's decking. My hands scrabble hopelessly in mid air, as I realise with horror that I am going over the side of the pier and into the ink-black water. My last focused thought as I fall is that it's still not past midnight – June 26th. The day I was supposed to have died isn't over yet. How could I have been so—

The sea is so cold that the pain of it makes me gasp. I feel like my thoughts and my heart are shutting down with the freezing shock. Trying to swim just makes me feel exhausted and weak, and the weight of my sodden clothes is dragging me down into the sea's black, icy depths.

As I surface I try to scream, but a wave washes over my frozen, upturned face and cold saltwater fills my mouth. My throat and lungs burn and my limbs feel tired and heavy. Another wave slaps against my face and I panic, cry and gargle water. As the cold bites and my strength fades, I realise I'm drowning.

My thoughts are jumbling, slipping away. I don't want to die. I want my mum. I want my gran. But there's only me, alone in the sea, drifting further away from the pier with every gasp.

Then, above the roaring in my ears, there's a distant, frantic yell. When I open my eyes, there's an orange life buoy ring floating near my head. But when I reach out and try to grab it with numb, useless fingers, it slips out of my hands and bobs away on a wave.

I scream again, but this time, it's a rage-filled scream. The feeling of helplessness has gone.

Pull yourself together, Lily McLean, I inwardly hiss. *You are not going to die here in freezing darkness, no way. You're wearing Mrs McKenzie's water lily charm. It will keep you safe. You owe it to Summer not to die tonight. She needs you. And Jenna needs you. Don't let her get thrown out of the house. And Bronx and Hudson need you. They'll forget the Three Unbreakable Rules. They'll get into trouble like their dad. And Mum needs you. Don't let your step-dad back into their lives.*

The life buoy ring is once again spinning through the air towards me. As it splashes in the water a short distance away, I gather all my strength and swim slowly, clumsily towards it. I reach out and clutch at its hard slippery sides. There's a moment of euphoria when I manage to grab the rope looped round it, then haul myself up, so my head and shoulders are out of the water. My body is floating, like a water lily in a pond, no longer drowning.

My eyes close as I feel myself being dragged through the rippling waves. All thoughts about being strong and keeping safe for my family's sake have evaporated. I'm shuddering with cold and tiredness and can't fight a moment longer. I need to sleep.

My sleep is disturbed by David, who is wrestling my body into the recovery position on the pier's wooden boards. I give in to an uncontrollable urge to vomit all the seawater I've swallowed. Rowan is crying hysterically. She would not make a good nurse.

"You'll be ok, Lily," says Aisha, sounding anguished. "The air ambulance is on its way. I'm so sorry. I'm sorry about everything. I'm an idiot. I've messed up so badly."

"Aisha, it was an accident. Stop this," barks David. "We need to focus on Lily. Can you hear me, Lil? It'll be all right. Can you hear the helicopter? It's coming for you."

I can't hear very well, for the buzzing in my ears. I try to shake my head, but can't seem to get it to move. I must tell David he should be a nurse or a paramedic when he leaves school, rather than a film director. He's good.

"Please forgive me, Lil. We are going to stay friends, aren't we, Lil? Please?" asks Aisha, clutching my hand. She is a real mixed-up kid, that one. I try and squeeze her hand, but I don't know if she can feel it. I am as weak and transparent as my ghost.

I close my eyes again, desperate for sleep.

Chapter 15

Reason to be happy:

★ I'm still alive... and that changes everything.

When I open my eyes a second time, everything looks different. The lights are so bright I have to blink furiously to focus. I am lying on a narrow bed, under starchy white sheets and a blue cotton blanket. There's a machine bleeping and I'm attached to it by a long snaking tube, which ends in the back of my hand. There are cartoon animals painted on every wall. I'm dead and I've gone to Disney hell.

"Hi Lily," says a gentle, familiar voice. I turn my head, which is aching, and see my mum standing by the bed. Her face is pale and tear-stained. "You're in hospital, dear."

My amazing powers of deduction have already worked that one out. I knew I wasn't dead really. My head and chest wouldn't be hurting so much if I was dead.

"The air ambulance brought you all the way to Glasgow. You're in Yorkhill Childrens' Hospital."

That explains the cartoon bunnies and the baby deer prancing all over the walls. Perhaps they should cater to different age groups in a children's hospital, rather than just the tinies. They could paint vampire murals for the teenage girls.

"The doctor says you are going to be absolutely fine. You have mild hypothermia, and you had a little water in your lungs, but you're a strong girl, aren't you?"

"Yes, Mum," I say, surprised by my whispery voice. "I think so." I try and sit up, but find that I can't, and so lie back down, exhausted. "Maybe not so much at the moment," I mumble.

"Your friends saved your life," Mum says. "They threw you the life belt and called the ambulance. Wasn't it lucky that they were there for you? You could have drowned..."

"Where are they?" I ask, eyes darting round the room, hoping to see them standing by my bed. I can imagine them there, David worriedly running his hands through his hair, Rowan tearful and relieved that I'm ok. And Aisha... I'm not so sure what Aisha would be doing. I don't know her well enough yet really. But I'm determined

I will, once we start secondary school in August. She clearly needs a friend.

"They are all at home with their parents. They've had a real fright," says Mum. I have a bad feeling that Rowan's mum is going to be even less keen than before about her associating with me. I'm clearly trouble.

Mum moves across the room, and opens the door.

"She's awake!" she calls, and there's a small cheer from outside the room. Gran comes shuffling in, her old face creased with fear and worry and I am sorry to have caused her such distress.

"Oh Lily," she sobs and envelops me in a huge bear hug. I think I'm suffocating. Then she towers over me, her face grim as a Viking shieldmaiden. "What were you thinking, leaving the caravan without telling me?" she roars. "I thought you were such a sensible child. You've let me down badly, Lily."

I flush with shame. I know exactly why I did it. I was trying to push aside my feelings, not wanting to be left alone with my thoughts, wanting to give my friends an exciting time and not thinking enough about my poor old gran.

"I'm so sorry, Gran," I whisper, my eyes flooding with tears.

"I think we should wait until Lily feels stronger before we badger her about how and why this happened," says Mum, calmly but firmly. Gran nods. They are for once in agreement.

They even give each other a big, tearful hug.

Jenna enters, carrying little Summer in her arms. Jenna's face is white and she looks exhausted.

"Silly cow," she says to me bluntly. "Don't you dare do anything so stupid again."

But she strokes my hair gently with her free hand and I see tears in her eyes. I'll need to have near-death experiences more often.

Wee Summer is clutching her scruffy toy lion and she grins when she sees me, oblivious to all the drama. I smile back at her, reach out and take her hand. She's real. She's my little sister, my ghost, my life saver. Summer senses that I'm not quite myself. She generously holds her lion out to me for a cuddle.

"Woawy," she says. "Woawy."

"I know," I say. "You've decided to call your lion Roary."

I take the scruffy little lion in my arms and hug him tightly. His fluffy mane tickles my nose.

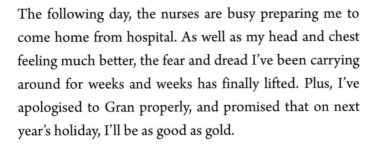

The following day, the nurses are busy preparing me to come home from hospital. As well as my head and chest feeling much better, the fear and dread I've been carrying around for weeks and weeks has finally lifted. Plus, I've apologised to Gran properly, and promised that on next year's holiday, I'll be as good as gold.

Mum and Gran are both in a particularly good mood today. While Gran and I were in Millport, the house was inspected by the council and they've agreed it's too small for our needs. We've been offered a bigger house nearby. Gran is planning to do her own inspection of it tomorrow. Maybe it's the thought of not having to share a bedroom with Bronx and Hudson any more that's making me so light-headed and dizzy.

I walk out into the sunny hospital corridor with its cheerful Lion King murals. *Keep them*, I think. We shouldn't ever grow out of liking kids' films. Who needs gloomy vampires?

My gran and my mum are coming along the corridor to meet me, both looking happy. Summer is waving at me from her pushchair. I wave back at her and laugh to myself. She has no idea what she has done for us.

"Wiwy come home," she shouts gleefully. I want to do cartwheels down the corridor. My wee sister speaks in sentences! She will have a wider vocabulary than Doug the Thug before the summer's out.

I want to get home, pack up all my stuff and move into our new place as soon as possible, because then I can invite my friends round whenever I want, though I might have to go round to Rowan's house first and grovel to her mum.

I'll need to convince Mum to take us all over to Millport for a day out so I can talk properly to Aisha. A trip to

Cumbrae will be good for Bronx and Hudson too. They need less television and more fresh air. And maybe we can persuade Jenna too, while she's still feeling grateful that I'm alive.

Most importantly, I owe Summer a big debt, and I plan on repaying it. I'm going to do the best I can to stick around. We may be a bit of a mixed-up family, but I know that together we'll be ok.

And as Aisha says, I also need to chill sometimes – I'm only eleven. I've got endless time, because, thanks to my baby sister, I'm still here.